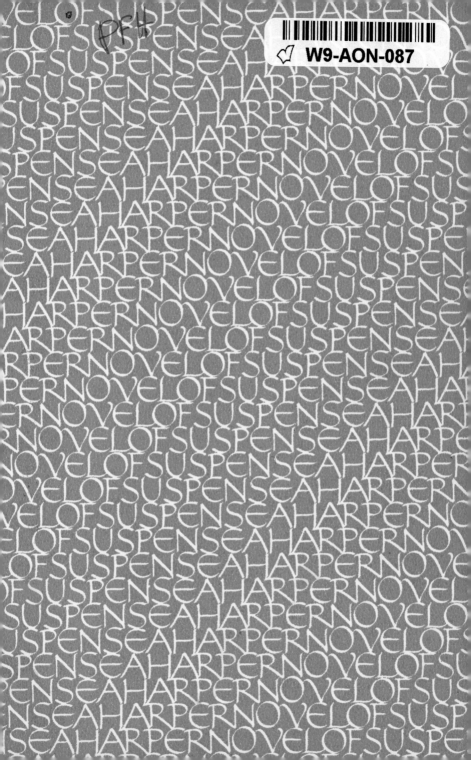

Bent Man

Books by Arthur Maling

Bent Man

Dingdong

The Snowman

Loophole

Go-Between

Decoy

Arthur Maling

BENT MAN

Harper & Row, Publishers

New York

Evanston

San Francisco

London

A HARPER NOVEL OF SUSPENSE

FIRST EDITION

Library of Congress Cataloging in Publication Data

Maling, Arthur.
    Bent man.
    I. Title.
PZ4.M25Be [PS3563.A4313]   813'.5'4   74–15878
ISBN 0–06–012802–X

75 76 77 78 79 10 9 8 7 6 5 4 3 2 1

For Skipper

Bent Man

1

I walked for a while. And wondered what the end would be like. I hoped it wouldn't be bad. I'd been afraid to ask.

I went into the bar in the Wrigley Building. I hadn't been there in years.

The bartender put down the jar of olives he was opening and came over to me.

"Martini," I said. "Straight up."

He nodded and mixed the drink. I watched him. He was an efficient bartender. "Has it started to snow yet?" he asked.

I shook my head.

He put the drink in front of me. "Paper says snow. Up to three inches."

I wanted to tell him that I didn't care about the snow. I wanted to tell him that I only had a few months to live. He was a stranger, though. I said nothing.

"You're in here all day, you don't know what the weather is like," he said.

I nodded.

He gave up trying to make conversation and went back to opening the jar of olives.

"I'd rather die in the spring," I said suddenly.

He looked up. "You say something?"

"Nothing," I said. Spring was a long way off. Chances were I wouldn't make it.

Two other men came up to the bar. They seated themselves a few stools away from me.

"Mr. Franken," the bartender said. "Mr. Wickes."

"Hi, Harry."

"The usual?"

"What else?" said Franken.

"Not me," said Wickes. "I'll have a Bloody Mary."

"Paper says snow," Harry told them.

"Feels like it," Franken said. He turned to Wickes. "Did you see the layout Burley did?"

"No," said Wickes.

"It stinks. That guy has to go."

"I've been saying that all along."

I wanted to tap Franken on the shoulder and say, Forget about Burley. Think about me. I just had a crazy experience. I found out I'm dying.

"I'd like to hire Garrison," Franken said. "He's good."

"Better than Burley, that's for sure. It'd be worth a try."

The bartender gave them their drinks. They went on about Burley and Garrison. I tried to relate to them. I couldn't. Not to Franken or Wickes or Burley or Garrison. Not to the bartender either. They were going to live, and I wasn't.

I paid for my drink and left.

It had started to snow.

2

Rita had put on a housecoat. She hadn't had time to button all the buttons, though. And she was in her stocking feet. "My goodness," she said.

"I thought I'd surprise you," I said.

"You certainly did." She presented her lips.

I kissed them. They were nice lips. Warm. I held her close for a moment. And tried not to drop the package.

"What's this?" she asked.

"Champagne."

"My goodness."

"We're having a party. Just for us."

She looked puzzled. "This is Thursday, isn't it?"

"This is Thursday." Usually I came over on Friday. Ours was a weekend-type love affair. Occasionally we also got together in the middle of the week, for something special. But not without talking it over first.

She smiled. "You sold a policy."

"I sold a policy," I lied. "A big one."

She threw her arms around me. "Darling!"

I felt a terrible sadness. "I also had an inspiration," I said.

"Well, don't just stand there. Take off your coat and tell me all about it. I want to hear everything. Every last detail. But first let me fix myself up. I'll be right back." She started for the bedroom.

I grabbed her and handed her the package. "Put this in the refrigerator on your way."

She left. I hung up my coat. I had my own corner in the closet. I loosened my tie.

Rita came back. She'd taken the bottle out of the bag and was holding it in her arms. The puzzled look had returned. "It's Bollinger," she said.

"Nothing but the best. I told you—it's a party."

She hesitated. "Is everything all right, Walter?"

"Of course everything's all right. I sold a policy. Now put that thing on ice before you drop it."

She walked slowly into the kitchen.

Christ, I thought. Oh, Jesus Christ!

I went into the living room and sat down. I avoided Walter's Chair and sat on the couch. The room was in a state of disorder. I liked it that way. On Friday nights it was always neat and by Sunday afternoons it was always a mess. The messiness gave me a feeling of accomplishment. I'd *been* there. I'd *used* things.

"Pour us something," Rita called from the bedroom.

"OK," I called back, and went into the kitchen. The kitchen was in better shape than the living room. Rita was meticulous about the kitchen, even on weekends. I took out ice cubes and glasses. "We're low on Scotch," I called.

Rita joined me. She'd taken off the housecoat she'd been wearing and put on the good one. The one I'd given her for her birthday. She'd also put on the gold mules. "I wasn't expecting you," she said. "I intended to buy some tomorrow."

I poured two small portions. That's all there was in the bottle.

"I wish I'd known you were coming," Rita said. "All I've got

4

in the freezer are a couple of Weight Watchers chicken dinners."

"What better way to celebrate?" I said. "Weight Watchers chicken dinners and champagne."

She smiled. "I love you very much. And I'm glad you're here. I just feel like a celebration. I really do."

I raised my glass. "To Weight Watchers."

Rita touched her glass to mine, and we drank. Then she giggled.

"What's so funny?"

"Us," she said, and giggled some more. "The way we're living our lives in reverse."

That was a favorite theme of hers. She often said that she felt younger now than she had at twenty, and whenever she said it I agreed that I did too. Which wasn't strictly true. Twenty had been my best age. I'd made All-American at twenty. But I had to admit that forty-two didn't seem particularly old. "Well," I said.

She became serious. "Walter."

"Yes?"

"Does life really begin at forty?"

I put down my glass. "What makes you ask that?"

"Because in two years that's what I'll be. And I'm skeptical."

"With a body like yours, honey, you have nothing to worry about." I grinned. "Especially if you stick with Weight Watchers."

"You just say that. I don't want to bag and sag and be ugly. You won't love me."

"I'll love you," I promised. Then it hit me again—the full impact of what Dr. Fenwick had said. I quickly picked up my glass and finished my drink.

"Are you all right, darling?"

"Sure I'm all right. Why do you keep asking?"

"You look pale, that's why."

"Come into the living room, and I'll tell you about my inspiration."

We went into the living room, but I didn't tell her about my inspiration. At least not right away. First Rita felt obliged to straighten things up. Then she had to see me properly installed in Walter's Chair—the chair I usually sat in. And she had to tell me the office news. She worked in the claims department at Old Settler, and it was a large department. Something was always happening. What had happened lately was that Felicia Viner, who had the desk across the aisle from Rita's, had announced that she was leaving, to have a baby, and what Rita wanted to tell me about was the shower that the girls were giving. She'd already mentioned the shower, but casually. Now she talked about it at length. How much the girls had collected. What they'd decided to buy: a playpen. This was far from the first such affair Rita had described to me, but for some reason it seemed to excite her more than any in the recent past.

I tried to appear interested.

"And now that I've got that off my chest," she said finally, "tell me about the policy you sold. Was it to Magnuson?"

"I thought you'd never ask," I said. "Yes, it was to Magnuson."

"Darling! I'm so happy for you!" She came over and kissed me. "Tell me everything."

I told her everything. It wasn't difficult. Eric Magnuson owned a chain of drugstores. I'd been trying for three years to sell him a major medical plan for his employees. I'd often talked to Rita about my attempts to close the deal. She knew almost as much about it as I did. But I went over the whole thing again. And manufactured a happy ending.

"See!" she cried. "You thought you'd never get a second big client. The next step is to sell him a pension plan."

"That's the next step," I agreed.

"You don't think the champagne will get too cold, do you?"

"I like it cold."

6

"I'd better turn on the oven, though. It's almost eight o'clock."

She turned on the oven.

"Now about my inspiration," I said when she came back. "Brace yourself."

She perched on the arm of my chair. Her expression was eager.

"We're going to take a vacation."

"Walter!"

"We're going to Jamaica. Just like we've always talked about."

"How absolutely fantastic!"

"And we're going strictly first class—Bollinger all the way. I'm going to make reservations tomorrow."

Her expression changed. Some of the glow disappeared. "To-morrow?"

"First thing in the morning. We'll leave just before the holidays."

The rest of the glow disappeared. "But we can't. I mean, I can't. Not over the holidays. It's a beautiful idea, darling, and you can't imagine how exciting I think it all is, but we can't go now. Maybe in March or April. Even that may be too soon."

"You've got vacation time coming, and you're going to take it. Now. Over the holidays."

She got up. She walked across the room. She fluffed up a pillow that she'd already fluffed up before. Then she came back. "You don't understand," she said. "Something exciting has happened to me too. I was saving it until tomorrow to tell you, but in the light of all this—"

"Yes?"

"Ann called last night. She's pregnant. I'm going to be a grandmother. Isn't that wonderful?"

I tried to think of something to say.

"So we can't go to Jamaica right now. I promised Ann I'd come to St. Louis for the holidays. She isn't feeling very well, and there's so much I can do. You understand, don't you? We can go to Jamaica in the spring, after the baby's born."

In the spring, I thought. "You'd better get the champagne out of the refrigerator," I said. "It's liable to get too cold."

And the next morning instead of going to the travel agency I went directly to my office. Where I found an FBI man waiting to see me.

3

He said that his name was Burr, and his identification card confirmed it. Edmund Burr.

"What can I do for you, Mr. Burr?" I asked, trying to sound better than I felt.

"I'd like to ask you a few questions, if you don't mind."

I looked at him. About my age, I thought. And like me, beginning to thicken in the middle. There was no hint of imminent unpleasantness in his appearance or his manner. "What about?"

"About your son."

I blinked.

"Your wife suggested that you might be able to help us."

I frowned. "My wife? I don't have a wife."

"Your ex-wife. Mrs. Livingston."

"Olive? That's the damndest thing I've ever heard."

Burr raised his eyebrows in polite surprise.

"I mean I haven't seen Steve in"—I tried to remember—"seven years. And I haven't seen his mother in seven years. And in case his mother didn't tell you, he isn't my son. Not legally, at any rate. Livingston adopted him years ago." Bitterness welled up as I spoke. I made an attempt to suppress it.

"Mrs. Livingston explained that."

"Then what the hell?"

"We have reason to believe that your son is in Chicago, Mr. Jackson."

I felt his eyes on me and wondered what he was seeing. "I didn't know that," I said.

He reached into an inside pocket and took out a photograph. He handed it to me. "This is a recent picture."

The paper wasn't the heavy, smooth kind that photographs are usually printed on. It was thinner, like the paper used in copying machines. It suggested that the picture was being widely distributed. The details weren't too sharp. There was no mistaking the subject matter, though. A fair-haired young man in swimming trunks standing with one arm around a girl, the other around a surfboard. The young man resembled me as I'd been at that age. Not as tall, not as beefy, but the same general appearance.

I felt a slight lump in my throat. "Is he a surfer?" I asked.

"A good runner too," Burr said.

I glanced at him.

He smiled. "I mean he was on the track team."

I nodded. "I was on the track team once. In high school."

"I know." There was kindness in Burr's voice. Also in his eyes. I got the idea that he liked me.

"I haven't seen the kid in so many years, I'm not sure I'd recognize him if I passed him on the street. He was only twelve." I studied the picture some more. "May I keep this?"

"Sure, Mr. Jackson."

I put it in my pocket. "Is Steve in trouble?"

"Yes and no."

Again I glanced at him. And again I found kindness in his eyes.

"I'm not being evasive, Mr. Jackson. He may be in trouble or he may not. He once was."

"I don't understand."

"He passed some bad checks. But his father—Mr. Livingston, I mean—made them good, and the charges were dropped. That's not what we're interested in at the moment. We're interested in the girl."

I took the photograph out of my pocket and studied the figure I hadn't paid much attention to before. She was very pretty. Beautiful, in fact. Dark hair, big eyes, a lovely body. "Who is she?"

"Her name is Georgette Himes."

"What's she done? Aside from going to the beach with my son, that is."

"She's part of a ring of jewel thieves."

I covered Steve and the surfboard with my thumb and concentrated on the girl. "A beautiful girl like that?"

"Yes, Mr. Jackson. She's a spotter."

"A spotter?"

"She watches the women in beauty shops. She spots the ones who wear expensive jewelry. She finds out about them. Then— well, pretty soon they don't have their expensive jewelry any more." He paused. "She has a very good eye, they say. She can tell a genuine diamond from an imitation a block away."

"Well, I'll be Goddamned. You aren't the only one who'd like to find her, I imagine. I can think of a few insurance companies who must share your interest."

"Naturally."

I gave the picture a final look and put it back in my pocket. "You think Steve knows where she is?"

"We think Steve is with her."

"I see."

He fumbled around inside his overcoat and found a package of cigarettes. He held it out to me. I took one. So did he. Then he fumbled some more and found a book of matches. He struck one and put it to the tip of my cigarette with great care, as if he wanted to do everything just right. Which made me wonder whether he thought I was withholding information. He lit his

11

own cigarette with less concentration and said, "We've traced them as far as Chicago. They arrived here two days ago."

"I see." I hoisted myself out of my chair and went to the window. I stood there, studying the view. It was a nice view for people who like air shafts. I myself didn't. But my window did face that of Charly Kipness, which was an advantage. On those occasions when both of us happened to look out at the same time we could signal whether we wanted to go down for coffee. Otherwise we had to use the telephone.

Charly was out at the moment. His office was dark. So I surveyed some of the other windows. I really didn't feel very well.

I turned back to face Burr and leaned against the wall. "Steve's mother doesn't know where he is?"

Burr shook his head. "She hasn't seen him in months. They're not on good terms, I take it."

"Yet she said that I might?"

"Well, when we mentioned Chicago—"

"We?"

"Our Los Angeles office."

"I get it. This is sort of a team effort."

"You might put it that way. After all, the FBI is a team."

"I didn't think she knew I was still here."

"She wasn't sure, as I understand it. But she thought that if you were—"

"She'd make life a little easier for me."

"Not exactly. But it's logical, in a way."

"Logical? It's not logical at all, Mr. Burr. Steve and I haven't had what you'd call a normal father-son relationship. I suppose you know that, but in case you don't I'll tell you. The last time I saw him, as I said, was seven years ago. He was twelve and he was in a boarding school in Santa Barbara. I hadn't had any luck getting to see him at home, so I decided to try the school. I had a big hassle with the principal—the headmaster, they call him. He didn't want to let me see Steve. I guess he'd been tipped off. Well, I wasn't taking no for an answer. I began to kick up a row and before I was through I made my point. Steve was brought into the office. He said some rather unflattering things to me and made it very clear that he didn't want to see me. Not then, not at any time in the future. A twelve-year-old kid, mind you. His own father. Well, that was that. I never tried again."

"Sometimes those things are for the best, Mr. Jackson. When a child has been adopted by his stepfather—"

"The hell you say! What would you know about it?"

"Are you all right, Mr. Jackson? You look pale."

"I'm all right. I got excited, that's all." I went to my desk and sat down. "But you get my point. It's not logical to assume that I'd know where Steve is."

"Are you sure you're all right?"

"Yes." I took a deep breath. "I'll be as frank as I can, Mr. Burr. I think I love Steve. You never stop loving your own child. I'm not sure, though. Sometimes I think you *do* stop loving them. If that's the case, then maybe I've stopped. But he hasn't been part of my life since he was a baby, and whenever I've tried to make him part of my life I've failed, and I hardly think I'll ever see him again. It isn't likely."

"Mr. Jackson—"

"Let me finish. I'm sorry that Steve is running around with a girl who's a spotter for some jewel thieves. I'm sorry and I'm surprised and I'm even kind of upset, I guess. When I looked at that picture . . . But at any rate, I'm sorry. I don't know how he came to be mixed up with anyone like that. He's had every advantage a kid can have. Every advantage that money can buy. His grandfather's one of the richest men in Southern California, and his stepfather's probably even richer. There's been money, money, money around since the day he was born. So his passing bad checks doesn't make sense to me, and neither does his getting mixed up with this girl, although that makes more sense, because she's gorgeous. But then, you never know with kids today, and I suppose that you have your facts straight. I'm sorry, and if I could help you I would, but—oh, shit, nothing ever works out the way it should, does it?"

"Mr. Jackson, I didn't mean to upset you."

I stubbed out my cigarette. Harder than was necessary. "What did you think you'd do?"

"All I want is the answers to a few questions."

"Well, ask them, then."

"The first you've already answered. You haven't heard from your son."

"Right."

"Do you know of anyone he might get in touch with here?"

"No."

"To your knowledge, has he ever been in Chicago before?"

"No."

"He's never tried to contact you?"

"I've already told you how things are. Do you mean to tell me that the FBI, with all its resources, traced them as far as Chicago and then—lost them?"

"The FBI, with all its resources, isn't infallible, Mr. Jackson. And Chicago's a big place."

"Right."

"One final question. You've already answered it, I think, but I'd like to make sure. You will cooperate with us, won't you? By that I mean if you do, by some chance, happen to learn of his whereabouts, you'll contact us? Let me give you my card."

I let him give me his card.

"There's always someone on duty," he said.

"Good for the FBI. What's your motto—'We always get our man'? Or is it 'Semper Fidelis'? No, that's the Marines."

"There's no need to get hostile, Mr. Jackson."

"I'm not hostile, Burr. This just isn't one of my better weeks. I'm sorry."

He hesitated. "Actually," he said, "I volunteered for this assignment." He sounded almost shy. A big man like that.

"I said I'm sorry. I mean it. I was out of line."

He swallowed. "I wanted to meet you."

My jaw didn't exactly drop. But it did go sort of slack. "You wanted to meet me?"

"Yes, sir. You see, I was at Southern Cal when you were, and

14

I—well, I admired you very much. You were the greatest running back we'd ever had. The greatest running back I've ever seen. The best there ever was. And that's not just my opinion. Then when you went pro I used to go to watch you whenever I could. In that game against the Packers—"

"An honest-to-God fan. Holy Toledo! I didn't think anyone remembered."

"Some of us do, Mr. Jackson. Some of us do."

"That was a long time ago, Burr."

There was a silence. I began to remember things that seldom came to mind any more.

"When I left the office I promised myself that I wasn't going to ask you this, Mr. Jackson, and I know I have no right to, and if you get mad I won't blame you, but all these years I've been wondering, and now that I'm here—well, what they said about you—that scandal—I mean, I didn't believe it was true at the time but I didn't really know."

I felt myself get red in the face. I stood up. "Yes, it was true," I said. "I was in with the gamblers. For five thousand dollars I threw a football game."

Burr looked disappointed and relieved at the same time. "Well, now I know."

"Now you know," I said, and suddenly my voice began to go out of control. "For five thousand dollars I threw a football game. Five thousand lousy dollars. And I'll tell you something else, something that maybe you don't know. I've paid for that mistake every day of my life since then, every day of my fucking life. I paid with my wife, I paid with my son, I paid with my job, I paid with every fucking thing I ever had, every fucking day of my life. I paid and paid and paid, and now that it's almost over—"

"Please. I didn't mean to upset you like this. I knew I shouldn't have said anything. I'm terribly sorry. It was none of my business. Let me get you a glass of water."

"I don't want a glass of water. I want you to get out of my office." I began to shake.

He jumped up and came over to me. "Please. Take it easy. I didn't mean—"

The shaking got worse. "Can't you understand English? Get out!"

He put his arm around me. "Take it easy. Jesus, is this all because of what I said?"

I pushed him away. "No," I rasped. "It's not because of what you said, you dumb, hero-worshiping son of a bitch. It's because I'm dying."

And for the first time since I was a child I began to cry.

4

Burr stayed with me for the entire morning, and then we had lunch together. I was feeling much better by that time.

We were no longer FBI agent and interviewee. We were no longer fan and fallen idol. We were friends.

Burr had put things into their proper perspective for me. The interview had been purely routine. He'd known in advance, through the checking done by the Los Angeles office, that there was little chance of my having seen or heard from Steve. He hadn't expected me to offer any more information than I'd offered. But someone had to ask. It was part of the job.

He'd also told me quite a bit about himself. Aside from the fact that he loved football, that is. He'd played tight end in high school and wanted desperately to go out for the team in college. But he'd received an academic scholarship and, having to maintain his grades, hadn't been able to afford the time for sports. He was a graduate lawyer but had never practiced law. He'd gone from law school right into the FBI and, except for a hitch in the Navy, had been in the FBI ever since. He'd lived in Los

Angeles, Seattle, Washington, D.C., and Chicago. He was married to a girl he'd met in Seattle, a clinical psychologist, and they had three children—two boys and a girl. The older boy was in college; the younger one and the girl were still in high school. His daughter was the brightest of the children and she had a special talent for acting. His wife had recently gone back to work and was happy with her job.

All in all, I concluded, Burr was not only a nice man, he was also a satisfied man. He liked his work and was devoted to his family, and if he sometimes wished that he could get a little more out of life than he was getting—well, who didn't?

But mostly we talked about me.

I told Burr things that morning which I'd never told anyone in my entire life. About my brother, for instance. My brother had been three years older than I, and much larger—I'd been small for my age. He'd bullied me, and I'd been afraid of him. Then when I was seven he'd been hit by a car and killed. I felt guilty, because I hadn't liked him. And right about then I began to grow. By the time I was ten I was half a head taller than any of the other children in my class at school. I felt guilty about that too. It seemed to me that I'd taken advantage of my brother's death by stealing some of his size. It was a crazy idea, entirely illogical, but for a long while I'd had it. Even now when I thought of my brother I had strange sensations of having done something wrong.

I told him about my father too. My father had been a coal miner. He'd been trapped for forty-eight hours by a cave-in which killed thirty men. He survived the cave-in but died six years later—of asthma. No one died of asthma, hardly. Not these days. But my father had, and I'd seen it happen. His death had affected me deeply, not only because it had come a year and a half after my brother's but because I'd been very fond of my father.

Even before my father's death my mother had drummed into me, and into my brother when he was alive, a hatred of mining. She'd grown up in Olyphant, Pennsylvania, in a family of miners

18

and had seen too many tragedies. She didn't have to stress it as much as she did—almost every kid I knew was getting the same indoctrination, and hatred of the mines was something we gave to one another. But my mother put everything she had into it. Boys who went to work in the mines were the boys who didn't do their homework, who had good voices but wouldn't sing in the choir, who didn't listen to their parents, who went to the movies and did foolish things. Practically everything she disapproved of led straight to the coal mines, and the coal mines were synonymous with hell. It worked, though. I didn't become a miner. I went to college. Because I was reasonably bright. Because I was an all-around good athlete. But primarily because I was good at football.

My mother could never make up her mind about football. It was one of the things that could lead a boy to the mines. On the other hand, when the principal of my high school began to make a fuss over me Mom conceded that maybe football was all right, and when people began to say that I was the best high-school back in the state of Pennsylvania she encouraged me with all the drive she'd once put into seeing that I studied my algebra. And when the word came through that I'd got the scholarship she wept with joy. Wept as she'd never wept before, even when my father died. The cycle had been broken. I was the first male member of her family since the family had come to America who wasn't going to be a coal miner.

It was one of the great satisfactions of my life that she got to see California. Six months before her death. She'd never been more than a hundred miles from Oliphant before. But they took up a collection at the high school I'd gone to, to buy her a plane ticket to Los Angeles. To watch me play in the Rose Bowl.

Looking back now, I explained to Burr, the college years had been the best years. But for a while I'd thought the years immediately after college were the best. I was married to Olive, we had a beautiful home, I had three good seasons in a row, and when people listed the top professional football players in the country my name was usually among the first five.

There were, of course, also some bad features to the post-college years. Such as Olive's family. Especially her father. He hadn't wanted her to marry me. I wasn't a native Californian, I wasn't rich, I was Catholic, I had no intention of becoming a banker—and he just plain didn't like me. He did everything possible to keep me from seeing Olive. But he couldn't lock her in her room and have her get the kind of education he believed in, so I did see her, and just before my graduation we eloped to Las Vegas. He refused to have anything to do with us after that. Olive's mother used to sneak over occasionally, but we never saw him. That suited me just fine, but it troubled Olive.

There was also a money problem. It seemed ridiculous, even to us, but it existed. What with my salary, speaking engagements and endorsements, I was earning around a hundred and twenty-five thousand dollars a year. But there was my agent to pay, there were taxes, and there was the house. With my bonus money we'd bought a four-hundred-thousand-dollar spread in Benedict Canyon, because at a quarter of a million it had seemed like a bargain, and the damn place kept us perpetually broke. And, oddly enough, to Olive the house was small. She was the daughter of O. J. Parkins and she'd never lived in anything that didn't require a permanent staff of eight. Having a permanent staff of two was quite a comedown.

Furthermore, she didn't like my football friends. She loved me enough to marry me in defiance of her father, but she couldn't understand why I preferred the kind of people I hung around with to the kind of people she'd always known. People who owned department stores and savings-and-loan companies and supermarket chains, or if they didn't own any of those things, were at least important in the film industry.

The problems were small, however, compared to the fun we were having. And if gradually I was slipping into debt, that wasn't serious. I had a lot of good years ahead of me.

Then, toward the end of our second year of marriage, Steve was born. That was the first really big problem we'd had to face. For he was malformed. His intestines, instead of being on the inside, were on the outside. It took six operations to make him normal. The operations were very expensive. And emotionally they made a wreck out of Olive.

I wanted to sell the house. She wouldn't consider that. A child needed room to play in. Five acres were barely enough. A child also needed a nurse, especially a child who'd been through all Steve had. So the staff of two became a staff of three. At which point I began to have dealings with the gamblers who'd been courting me all along. Betting on games. Other games, at first. Then the games I was playing in. Winning some bets, losing others, but losing more than I was winning.

It was almost inevitable that eventually I'd take a bribe. And eventually I did. I suppose it was also inevitable that sooner or later I'd get caught. Well, that happened too. Sooner rather than later. The very first time I did it.

The team almost lost its franchise. I almost went to jail. It cost my father-in-law a hundred thousand dollars in lawyers' fees and incidentals to keep me from being convicted. He didn't do it for me, he declared; he did it to protect his daughter's name and his own. At any rate, I didn't go to jail. All that happened was that I got permanently suspended. I would never again be able to do the one thing I was really good at: play football. Not professionally. And I didn't know how else to earn a living.

There'd been a lot of people who wanted to take me in as a partner in one business or another, before. There'd been a lot of people who were willing to pay to have me say nice things about their products. Now all of those people seemed to vanish into thin air. I couldn't even get them to return my telephone calls. I finally wound up on the payroll of a sporting-goods store where my main function was to stand around and let the customers look at me.

I studied for the insurance exam and passed it. But all the good folks who bought insurance in large amounts already had insurance brokers. Especially, it seemed, the friends of O. J. Parkins, or anyone who had any dealings with O. J. Parkins—which included almost everyone in the state who had big money. O. J. Parkins did everything possible to make things tough for me, with the exception of putting pressure on the insurance board to prevent my getting a license. He might as well have done that too, though, for all the good the license did me.

The house went. The nurse went. Olive went.

Olive didn't go until after she'd had a nervous breakdown that put her in the hospital for two months. By then I was willing to concede that maybe a divorce would be the best thing. Her father would be glad to have her back as long as I didn't come with her. She'd be comfortable. Steve would have all the things a kid needed. I'd get by somehow.

We were divorced in the same town where we'd been married. Las Vegas.

What I'd have done if it hadn't been for Ben Small I don't know. But just when I was at my lowest ebb, when I was convinced that I didn't have a friend in the world, I found that I did have one. A true friend.

I'd met Ben when both of us were in our second year at Southern Cal. We were in the same chemistry section. Chemistry was more his thing than it was mine. Which figured. His father was chairman of the board of Carling-Small Laboratories, which had an annual volume of just under a billion. Ben helped me with problems and experiments that were beyond me, and we became friends. We remained friends until graduation. Then he went home to Chicago and to the job of learning how to run Carling-Small. Except for a few Christmas cards I hadn't heard from him since.

But six months after Olive and I were divorced I met him one Sunday morning on Wilshire Boulevard. He was in town for a sales meeting. We talked.

He didn't care about the scandal or the suspension or any other damn thing. We'd been friends and he'd liked me and he still liked me, and that was that.

By Tuesday night I was on the plane with him, bound for Chicago.

He helped me find an apartment. He supported me during the period it took me to get my insurance license in Illinois. He gave me a chunk of the Carling-Small insurance business. The commissions on that chunk amounted to ten thousand a year.

I still had that portion of the Carling-Small insurance which he'd thrown my way. I'd picked up some other customers too. No big ones, but quite a few small ones. Enough to keep me going.

Ben and I didn't see each other often. He now had the job which had formerly belonged to his father. He was chairman of the board. His life was very complicated. There were houses in Lake Forest and in Palm Beach, and there were meetings and conferences all over the world. Not just business conferences. Ben was interested in a lot of other things too. Environmental protection, a couple of hospitals, half a dozen boys' clubs and any number of organizations that had to do with public health. Every now and then, though, busy as he was, he called me. Everything all right? Sure, Ben. How about getting together for lunch tomorrow? Love to, Ben.

Once a friend, in Ben's case, always a friend.

"Does he know you're dying?" Burr asked.

I shook my head. "No one in the world knows. Just you and me and a couple of doctors. I'd like to keep it that way for a while."

"What about Rita?" Burr asked. I'd told him about her too.

"I'd like to spare her as long as I can."

"Eventually she'll have to know, Walter."

"Eventually."

Burr stared at the tabletop. "Isn't there *anything* they can do?"

"A little. I haven't told Rita yet but I'm going into the hospital Sunday night for three days, to get these shots. Nitrogen-mustard shots, they're called. That will make the thing regress temporarily." Nitrogen mustard. It sounded like something you'd put on a plastic hotdog. But it would give me life for a few months.

"I can't believe it."

"Neither can I. And what makes it so crazy is that I don't feel all that sick. I didn't before and I don't now. I don't feel all that well, I admit, but I don't feel all that sick either."

"You felt sick enough to go to the hospital."

"No. I felt sick enough to go to the doctor. The doctor's the one who put me in the hospital. Just for tests, he said. He wasn't satisfied with my blood count, he said. He didn't say anything about that funny swelling. Just the blood count. He wanted to give me some more tests and call in a hematologist, he said. So I went."

"I didn't know you before, Walter, but you don't look so bad to me. Pale, maybe, but what the hell."

"I know. Every now and then I wasn't feeling well. Not really sick but definitely not well. Like I was running a fever. Finally I took my temperature and found that I *was* running a fever. Nothing else. Just a fever. Then a few weeks ago I noticed this swelling under my right armpit. I didn't relate it to the fevers. I didn't relate it to anything. But I decided to have a checkup. The finding: Hodgkin's Disease."

Burr looked at me. "I'm not a doctor, Walter, and I don't have all the answers. But I've heard of people with Hodgkin's Disease who've lived for a long time and even been cured."

"So have I, Ed. And that's what the doctor said. You can be cured by radiation. But not in my case. The liver's involved, and they can't radiate the liver."

"Oh."

There was a long silence. Finally Burr said, "I suppose you and he have considered every possibility."

"I was in his office for an hour and a half yesterday. He kept all of his other patients waiting while we went over it. The answer: Hodgkin's Disease with enlarged lymph nodes and liver involvement. Shots. Remission. Final curtain."

There was another long silence.

"Will Rita look after you?" Burr asked.

"If I want. She doesn't know I had an appointment with

Fenwick yesterday. She knows I was in the hospital, of course, but I told her the day I came out that everything was all right, because I really thought it was. Dr. Nicholson—the hematologist who made the tests—he told Fenwick what the score was but he didn't tell me. All he told me was that I'd better see Fenwick as soon as possible, which was probably a good thing. I've known Fenwick for years. It was better getting the news from him. But at any rate Rita believes what I myself believed until yesterday, and I'm happy about that. The next few months would be pure hell for both of us if she knew the truth."

"But you're going to need care, Walter."

"Not for a while. And when that time comes—well, I don't know. Rita's had a hard life. I don't want to make it any harder for her than I have to. So maybe I'll just go away someplace. Dying is something you kind of have to do by yourself anyway."

"I'd really like to look in on you every now and then, if you wouldn't mind."

"It would be a pleasure. I'm sorry that we're getting acquainted so late in the game."

"Better late than never," Burr said. "The wife and I would be happy to have you and Rita out for dinner. Maybe one night next week."

"Swell. As soon as I get out of the hospital."

"I'll call you."

He signaled for the check and paid it. And with renewed promises that we'd see each other soon we parted.

I went back to my office. It had been a strange twenty-four hours.

5

We went to the movies that night. There was a picture at the Esquire that Rita had been wanting to see. Donald Sutherland was in it, and Rita had a thing about him.

After the movie we went next door to The Pickle Barrel for coffee, and I broke the news about going to the hospital on Sunday. For more tests, I said.

"But you were just there," she said. "Everything's all right, you told me."

"It is," I said. "This is for my neck. I talked to Fenwick today. He thinks they may be able to do something about it." I'd been having trouble with my neck for several years. There was a narrowing of the space between a couple of the vertebrae, which put pressure on a nerve. It wasn't serious but from time to time it hurt a lot. There wasn't much that could be done about it.

"For that you have to go to the hospital?"

"Only for three days. I'll be out on Wednesday."

Rita said nothing. She looked skeptical, though. Finally she said, "I'm sorry about Christmas, Walter. Would you like to come down to St. Louis with me? Ann and Nils would love to have you."

"I don't think so."

"Why not? It would be nice."

There was no special reason. I was very fond of Ann. Also of Julie, Rita's younger daughter. And Nils was my type of guy. "I don't know. What's Julie going to do?"

"I haven't told her about Ann yet. She'll probably come to St. Louis for a few days. And Terry wants her to go skiing with him."

"I'm not in favor of that." Terry Avalon was Julie's boyfriend. He was definitely not my type of guy. He had what I called a big-shot syndrome.

"I didn't think you would be."

The waitress refilled our coffee cups.

I caught Rita eyeing me.

"Walter," she said.

"Yes?"

She changed her mind. "Nothing." Then she changed it back again. "We've never lied to each other, have we?"

Oh, Lord. "Sure we have. We lie to each other constantly."

"No we don't. But I have the feeling at the moment—"

"Cut it out, Rita."

"I have the feeling at the moment that you're not telling me the truth. You have something on your mind."

I didn't know what to say. She had her share of perceptiveness. Unless diverted, she'd eventually come up with the right answer. "A peculiar thing happened today," I said.

"I thought there was something. What happened?"

"A fan of mine caught up with me. A fellow who was at Southern Cal when I was. He's an FBI agent now. Swell guy. He invited us for dinner next week. From the way he talks, his wife is a good cook."

"Do you want to go?"

"Maybe. We'll see."

"Where did you run into him?"

"He came to my office."

Rita raised her eyebrows inquiringly.

I told her about Steve.

She was shocked.

We batted the subject around for a while. I showed her the picture of Steve and Georgette Himes. She studied it. She agreed that Georgette Himes was extremely pretty. Her main interest was in Steve, however. She'd never seen a picture of him, because I'd never before had one. She kept looking from the picture to me and back to the picture. "There really is a resemblance," she said. "Is that what you were like at that age?"

"Sort of. I was bigger and not as blond and I didn't have that sort of trim look, but yes, I guess you could say that's what I was like."

"You were handsome."

"I'm still handsome."

Rita smiled.

I paid the check, and we left. The three inches of snow which had been forecast had fallen. The streets were slippery. We didn't get back to Rita's apartment until almost midnight. And when we did get there we found that we had unexpected company. Julie. She'd come up from Champaign for a day. She'd got lonesome, she said.

We sat up for a long time, talking. Julie was in her second year at the University of Illinois. She loved the school and was doing well. Julie was the sort of girl who usually did well at everything.

Rita told her about the baby that was on the way, and Julie was overwhelmed by the prospect of becoming an aunt. She wasn't overwhelmed by the prospect of spending Christmas in St. Louis, however. She pointed out, with the logic that was typical of her, that it didn't seem right to give Ann extra work at a time when she wasn't feeling well. But Rita replied, with the logic that was typical of *her*, that *she* was the one who'd be doing the work—that was why she was going. Julie finally agreed that she'd go to St. Louis for four days. Then she planned to meet Terry in Boyne, Michigan.

I frowned. "How are you going to get there?"

Julie shrugged. "I'll find a way."

"There's an energy crisis."

"Terry has plenty of energy," she informed me with a grin.

I continued to frown. I supposed I was wrong. Terry was attractive enough, and bright. But I just didn't approve of him, or of any young man of twenty who flew to Las Vegas for weekends, wore jackets with velvet collars and sported diamond rings.

Julie came over to me. "Don't look like that," she said. "Terry's really very nice." She kissed me lightly on the forehead.

"It's none of my business anyway," I said.

"Sure it's your business," Julie said. "You're my weekend father. But you just don't understand Terry."

"He reminds me of certain types I used to know," I said. But I stopped frowning. I liked the weekend-father bit. It had its origin in the days when Rita and I were forming our relationship. Julie and Ann were in their early teens then. Both Rita and I worried about the effect our sleeping together might have on them. We went to a lot of trouble to give the impression that we were just friends. Tiptoeing around. Whispering. Getting out of bed at three in the morning so that I could drive her home from my place or sneak out of hers. We thought we were being very clever, until one day the girls approached us and said they wished we'd quit acting so adolescent and admit that we were lovers. That cleared the air, which was further cleared when Ann, with a maturity that sat oddly on her young soul, said, "If Mother can't have a real husband, and if we can't have a real father, at least we can have a weekend substitute." And they began to call me their weekend father.

I tried to live up to the role. I was still hoping, in those days, that Rita would come around. I wanted her to divorce her husband, marry me and take me into her life on a full-time basis. She hadn't, and I knew now that she never would. But for a number of years I'd lived with the belief that she would. She loved me and swore that I was the only man except her husband she'd ever slept with, which I believed. Yet she refused to have me on more than a part-time basis.

At one time or another I'd come up with various theories. Eventually I narrowed them down to just one. She'd had a rotten marriage. Her husband had been in the Regular Army. They'd had a good life for a number of years. Then he began to go insane.

He hadn't gone insane all at once. He'd gone insane by degrees, over a period of time. There were ups and downs. Hope followed by despair. But a gradual slipping. Rita had never told me all of it but she'd told me some of it. The violent rages, the periods of placidity, the attempt on her life—he'd tried to strangle her in her sleep one night.

Now he was in an Army hospital. He'd never come out. He was a paranoid schizophrenic. But she wouldn't divorce him.

My theory was that her marriage had left her with a fear of marriage in general. And as long as she was legally bound to Joe Swift she couldn't marry anyone else. So she invented her own code, and both of us lived by it.

It was three o'clock before we got to bed.

And we were up early, because Terry came by to pick up Julie. They were going over to his place, they said.

After they left, Rita and I had a leisurely breakfast, then went to the grocery store. We usually did our marketing together, on Saturday mornings. Rita had a standing appointment at the beauty shop on Saturday afternoons, and while she was having her hair done I either called on clients whom I hadn't been able to see during the week, or just puttered around. Sometimes I did my puttering at her place, sometimes at mine.

On that particular Saturday I went to mine. For while we were at the grocery store I'd begun to feel ill.

6

I'd taken to leaving the thermometer on the night table. I used it now. I had a temperature, all right. Slightly over a hundred and one.

I stretched out on the bed and consoled myself with the thought that after I had the shots the fevers would stop. For a while, anyway.

I began to enumerate the things that had to be done. The main thing was to arrange to turn my business over to someone. At times I'd thought of taking in a partner but I'd never connected with the right person. I still didn't have anyone particular in mind, but Charly Kipness was a possibility. He wasn't the most energetic man I'd ever known but in his own way he was conscientious, and he could certainly use a few new clients—he was struggling. He'd probably lose the big client. Ben Small would give the Carling-Small business to someone else. But Charly would keep some of the lesser clients, and every little bit helped.

I was sorry now that I hadn't been more energetic myself. I could have built a better business than I had. From time to time I'd tried. I'd just never tried hard enough. Like with Magnuson. Somewhere along the line I should have been able to close that deal. I simply hadn't put enough into it. Was it laziness? Or had I simply not cared?

Perhaps neither. Perhaps I'd simply chosen to punish myself.

Charly Kipness would be grateful. All I had to figure out was how to tell him one thing without telling him the other.

I also had to make a will. I'd never considered that I'd had much need for one. No family, no money. But that wasn't quite true. I did have money. About sixteen thousand dollars, if my estimate was correct. Plus whatever the furniture and car were worth. Eighteen or nineteen thousand altogether. And I did have a family. Or did I? I'd have to look into that. If I died without a will, would Steve inherit or wouldn't he? Legally he wasn't my son. Actually, it didn't matter, though. Someday he'd be worth millions, if he wasn't worth millions already. Another few thousand wouldn't mean anything to him. But whether it did or not, I wanted to make sure that he'd have no claim. I wanted everything to go to Rita. The few thousand that wouldn't mean anything to Steve would mean a lot to her.

I'd been a damn fool to agree to let Livingston adopt Steve. I certainly hadn't had to. I'd thought I was doing the right thing. Olive had made a special trip to Chicago. Her father had come with her. For the first time in all the years I'd known him O. J. Parkins made an attempt to be civil to me.

The things they said made sense, too. Since his mother now had the name Livingston, it would be less confusing to the boy if he had that name too. After all, he was six years old. He was already asking questions. Furthermore, Livingston had no children of his own and wasn't likely to have any by Olive— she didn't want any more children. Steve would be Livingston's heir. And what good did it do me to go on being Steve's father when he lived in California and I lived in Chicago?

It all made sense.

What I hadn't thought of was that Steve would feel that I'd deliberately deserted him. And that he'd be told about the football scandal over and over again. A father who'd deserted him. A father who was a crook.

Nor had I thought that when I did want to see him Olive would make it impossible.

No doubt about it: I'd been a fool. Or had I been trying in still another way to punish myself?

The business. A will. What else was there? Not much, really. I certainly hadn't lived a complex life. Merely a self-lacerating one.

What would Rita think if I went to Jamaica by myself? All the wrong things, I supposed. Or worse yet, the right ones.

Jamaica, of all places. Why did I think it was so important to see Jamaica? A pretty island, no doubt. But no prettier than many others. It was just one of those things. For years I'd wanted to go there. For years Rita and I had talked about it. Something had always come up, though. Except for a few days once, when we'd gone to the Wisconsin Dells, Rita and I had never taken a trip together.

Still, it was nice that Ann and Nils were going to have a baby. They'd make good parents.

The doorbell rang.

It can't be Rita, I thought. She never gets through at the beauty shop until at least four.

Julie, probably. But why would she come here?

Wearily I got off the bed.

The doorbell rang again. I'm coming, I told it.

I went into the hall and pushed the button that unlocked the downstairs door. Then I opened the door of my apartment and waited.

I recognized him the moment he stepped out of the elevator.

He came across the corridor to where I was standing.

I stared at him, unable to find words.

"You probably don't remember me," he said. "It's been such a long time. I'm Steve—your son."

I nodded. Finally words came. Three of them. "I remember you," I said.

7

I'd lived through the scene many times in my fantasies. In some of the fantasies I'd been kind and forgiving. In others I'd been cold and bitter. But in none of them had I been tongue-tied.

And that was what I was. I just couldn't get my vocabulary together. Not during the first few minutes, at any rate.

Steve seemed a bit uncertain too. Less so than I, however. He looked around the living room with obvious interest and admired the view of Lincoln Park. He commented on a couple of the prints on the wall and a book that happened to be on the sofa. All of his reactions were positive. His reaction to me seemed to be positive too. There was certainly no trace in him now of the angry adolescent who'd turned his back on me in Santa Barbara. This was an adult. One with friendly eyes and a nice smile.

"It's not what I pictured," he said finally. "Neither are you."

"Well, after all," I said.

He didn't pursue that line. "I read something about you recently," he said.

I nodded.

He didn't pursue that line either. "Look," he said. "The last time I saw you I acted like an awful brat. I felt bad about it afterwards."

"That's all right," I said.

"I was really rotten, I'm afraid."

I shook my head.

"I've thought about it a lot."

"Coffee?" I said. "Or maybe a drink?"

"I suppose you were pretty mad at me."

I shrugged.

"I don't blame you."

I tried to smile.

"Scotch, if you have it."

"I have it." I went into the kitchen and busied myself with ice and glasses.

When I returned to the living room Steve was again looking out of the window. I studied his back for a moment. He was taller than he'd appeared in the photograph. And blonder. And broader across the shoulders. He was too thin, though.

I felt an enormous rush of tenderness. It startled me.

He turned around and caught me gazing at him. "I haven't often seen snow," he said. "It's pretty."

"I know." I put the glasses down. I'd forgot to bring the Scotch.

I went back for it.

"Have you lived in this apartment long?" he asked when I returned.

"Five years," I replied, handing him one of the glasses.

"Five years," he repeated thoughtfully, as if he was trying to relate those five years to his own life.

"Cheers," I said.

"Cheers."

36

I began to regain my self-possession. "You've grown a bit, it appears."

He grinned.

"When did you get to town?"

"Just a few days ago." He paused. "I would have called you right away, but to tell the truth I was scared." He paused again. "I still am, a little."

"There's nothing to be scared of."

"I don't know. I acted so lousy and—I don't know—what it is, I think, is I thought a lot of things that weren't so nice, and then I was ashamed of them, and then I thought them again. I know I'm not making much sense."

"You're making sense. But there's nothing to be scared of."

He gave a very deep sigh. "These things I read about you. They said you were very good."

"Where did you read them?"

"In the library. I mean, I went there to see if they had anything. They had quite a bit. In old newspapers and magazines."

"You went to the library to read about me?"

"Well, how else was I going to find out?"

I said nothing. He'd read the bad along with the good, no doubt.

"It was very exciting, actually. I never knew you were one of the All-Stars."

"I had my moments. Good and bad."

"Are you disappointed?"

"Disappointed?"

"That I didn't turn out to be a football player."

That was the last thing I would have expected him to have on his mind. And it was certainly the last thing I'd thought about in connection with him. "No."

"I'm not much of an athlete, I'm afraid."

I recalled what Burr had told me. A good runner; on the track team. And I recalled the surfboard. "Really?"

"I made the varsity track team, but that was because there

was no competition. Everybody who went out for track was on the varsity team."

"Well."

"I won a few races, though."

"That's good."

"Are you really not disappointed, or are you just saying that?"

"I mean it."

He heaved another of those deep sighs.

"What sort of aptitude have you for girls?" I asked.

He smiled broadly. "No problems there." His smile faded. "Why do you ask?" He sounded genuinely puzzled. Apparently my wondering about girls struck him as oddly as his wondering about football had struck me.

"Well, you're at that age."

He laughed. "I've been at that age for a long time."

I laughed too. And felt another rush of tenderness. It was so intense that it stopped my breath for a moment. When it had passed I said, "It's good to see you, Steve," and finished my drink in one gulp. "Tell me about yourself."

"Well, I'm six-one. I weigh—"

"I don't mean that. What are you doing in Chicago?"

"Floating."

"Floating?"

"I'm a very good floater." His expression changed. It became serious. "I'm not doing anything."

I waited for him to go on.

He did. "Father threw me out. Mother helped him. So I'm not doing anything."

"Threw you out?"

"I'm a disgrace to the family."

Once more I waited for him to go on, but this time he didn't. "If there's any more Scotch left," he suggested.

I refilled his glass and my own. Neither of us spoke for a while. "Do you have any money?" I asked finally.

"Some. I didn't come here to put the bite on you, if that's what you're thinking."

"That wasn't what I was thinking. However, if you need some—"

"I don't."

He didn't appear to, either. He was dressed in casual clothes. But the loafers were from Gucci, the turtleneck was of cashmere and the leather jacket was similar to one I'd seen for three hundred dollars. "OK," I said.

He went off on a different tack. "You know what I was thinking? I was thinking you'd probably be married."

"Well, I'm not."

He considered that. He pointed to a picture of Rita which stood on one of the end tables. "The woman over there—?"

"A friend."

He nodded understandingly.

I thought of the picture in the pocket of my jacket. I wondered how I was going to get around to the subject of Burr and Georgette Himes. This certainly wasn't the time for it. Later, perhaps. I could take him out to dinner, we could have a long talk—

The doorbell rang.

"I'll be Goddamned," I said. And immediately I began to get nervous. I made no move to push the button.

The doorbell rang again.

"You're expecting company?" Steve asked.

"That's the funny thing. I'm not." Could it be Burr? It could be anyone. Not Burr, though. Not so soon.

The doorbell rang for the third time.

"You'd better answer it," Steve said.

I decided that it positively couldn't be Burr. I went to the hall and pushed the button.

It wasn't Burr. It was Julie. With Terry Avalon.

"I'm sorry if I woke you up," Julie said, "but I left my key at home and I'm locked out. Can I borrow yours?"

"Sure, honey." I reached into my pocket.

"Nice place you have here," Terry said.

I glowered at him. He hadn't even seen it yet—he was still

standing in the corridor. "Thanks," I said.

"Let me show you around," Julie told him. "The view is super."

"Wait a minute," I protested, but she was already brushing past me, leading Terry by the hand.

Julie stopped when she saw Steve. She turned to me. "Oh," she said, "I didn't know you had company. I'm sorry if I interrupted something."

I'd intended to introduce him as a client, but before I could say anything Steve spoke. "Hi," he said, giving Julie a cordial smile. "I'm Steve Livingston."

Julie, who knew about him, gaped. Terry, who didn't, said "Hi."

Julie turned to me. Her eyes were a pair of enormous question marks.

"He just came into town," I said.

"I dig that jacket, man," Terry told him. Evidently he too had priced one like it.

Steve nodded but he kept his eyes on Julie. She turned from me to him, and when she found him staring at her she blushed.

"It really is a nice place," Terry said, looking around. He was only a couple of inches shorter than Steve and was well put together. But somehow, in the comparison, Terry didn't come off so well. Partly because of his clothes, partly because of his expression. He was wearing a suede jacket with a Persian-lamb collar, plaid slacks with three-inch cuffs and two-toned shoes, the tones being green and maroon. Plus the diamond ring, of course. And his expression was too frankly appraising. He was studying to become an accountant, and he was apparently very good at whatever it took to become one—he had a 3.7 average at Northwestern. But he wasn't an accountant yet, and I hadn't invited him in to determine the value of my personal property. That's what he appeared to be doing, however.

"We'd better be going," Julie said, pulling Terry toward the door.

"So soon?" Steve asked.

40

"I think you'd better be," I agreed.

Terry continued with his inventory as Julie led him away. There was a flurry of good-byes, and I quickly closed the door.

"Pretty girl," Steve remarked.

"She's the daughter of the woman in the picture over there."

"No kidding?"

I suddenly decided that I'd better not wait to straighten things out; I'd better do it now. "Sit down, Steve."

We went over to the couch. I hastily assembled my thoughts.

"There's something I have to tell you," I said. "A man from the FBI came to see me yesterday. He wanted to ask me some questions. About you."

8

Delmore Livingston had inherited the Livingston Ranch. The Livingston Ranch was a nice piece of property. At one time it had been in the country, but Greater Los Angeles had engulfed it. No one really knew what it was worth now, since the land had been subdivided for commercial and residential purposes. The last figure I'd heard was a hundred and thirty million, but that was some years back; at this point it was probably worth considerably more.

Delmore Livingston also had inherited a little acreage near Long Beach. No one knew what that was worth either, but they'd been pumping oil out of it for thirty-five years.

Delmore Livingston was a son of a bitch, though.

Dignified, charitable to the right charities, advisor to senators and cabinet members, patron of all the more acceptable arts. But a son of a bitch.

At least according to Steve. And I was inclined to believe him. Firstly, because I'd heard rumors to that effect when I was living in Southern California. Secondly, because anyone whom

42

O. J. Parkins approved of had to be a son of a bitch.

Livingston had provided Steve with a good home, if by good you mean large. He'd provided him with a good education, too, if by good you mean expensive. Also with other advantages—clubs, camps, contacts. The only thing Livingston hadn't given the kid was love. In fairness to him, I guessed that he'd wanted to, but the feeling just wasn't in him. Steve was his wife's son, not his. And Livingston was evidently a man who, through no fault of his own, was all locked up inside of himself. He'd adopted Steve because he'd thought it was the right thing to do, and because he'd liked the image of himself as a father. But he'd probably been regretting for years that he'd done so.

As for Olive, Steve's relationship with her had been nothing short of tempestuous. Why—I didn't know, and Steve couldn't explain. It had something to do, I supposed, with the fact that she'd married Livingston.

Steve had been chauffeured around in a Rolls-Royce for years but had never had more than ten dollars in his pocket. Rich boys, Livingston believed, had to learn the value of money the same as poor boys did. The trouble was, most poor boys had more money to experiment around with than Steve had had. It got so bad that he finally began to chisel. To buy things at various stores, charging them to his mother's account, then return them for cash. His mother caught on after a while and put a stop to the practice. So he passed some bad checks. Sixteen hundred dollars' worth in one week. That's all the time he'd had. Livingston had been notified, and there'd been a terrible rhubarb. As a result of the rhubarb Steve had left the Livingston domain—left or been thrown out, depending upon which part of the shouting one happened to have heard.

There'd been no contact between Steve and the Livingstons since then. Or, for that matter, between Steve and his maternal grandparents, who'd come to the conclusion that he was simply a chip off the old block—the old block being me.

So Steve took up residence with the older brother of one of his classmates. Not a bad residence, either. A five-room beach house with glass walls, sliding doors and a wet bar in the living room. The older brother only used the place part of the time; he also had an apartment in Westwood. But people came and went. Some stayed for a few hours, others for weeks. It didn't seem to make any difference whether the host was present or not—there was always plenty to eat and plenty to drink and plenty to smoke, and the party just continued, with an ever changing assortment of guests. In a way, Steve pointed out, life at the beach house had given him a better education than college would have done. And in a way I had to agree with him. But only in a way.

It was while staying at the beach house that he met Georgette. She came with a group one Saturday afternoon and stayed until Monday morning.

She wasn't the first girl in his life. There'd been a wide selection of them ever since he'd arrived at the beach house. A virtual smorgasbord of attractive women. And even before that he'd had a number of females on the string. What Georgette was was the most interesting.

She was separated from her husband but not divorced. Her husband was an ex-policeman. At various times, to make ends meet, she'd done bit parts on television, hustled hamburgers and milkshakes at a drive-in restaurant, manicured fingernails in a beauty shop and sold cosmetics in a department store. She was as bright as she was beautiful and she was the kind of woman who, no matter how she got bounced around, managed to come up undamaged.

Steve fell in love with her.

It wasn't until later that he learned she wasn't the twenty-three she claimed to be but was twenty-eight. Or that although she was separated from her husband she still saw him frequently. But by then such things no longer mattered—he was in love.

As I listened to Steve's account of the relationship I tried to see him as the innocent victim of an unscrupulous older woman. To an extent I could. He was innocent. She was older. And she was without doubt unscrupulous. What threw everything out of kilter, however, was the fact that while Georgette was unscrupulous she hadn't been unscrupulous with Steve. She had, apparently, fallen as much in love with him as he had with her. She did things for him that cost her time and money even though there was no benefit to herself. She bought him clothes. She took him into her apartment and cooked for him and made an effort to pursue whatever activities interested him. If anyone had been getting the short end, it was Georgette, not Steve.

"Sounds to me like you were a kept man," I said with a frown.

"Well, not exactly," he replied. "I had a couple of jobs."

"What kind of jobs?"

"Well, I worked for a while behind the lunch counter at this drugstore. Then I hiked cars in a garage."

"Did you hike cars in your Gucci loafers?"

"No, I—"

"And did you know that your girlfriend was working for a ring of jewel thieves?"

That was the big question, and he treated it accordingly. He didn't answer.

I waited.

He still didn't answer.

"Steve," I said at last, "I'm going to be truthful with you. For a long time I wondered whether I loved you or not. I occasionally thought I didn't. I was mad as hell at you. Now that I'm in the same room with you I know that I'm not mad any longer and I never stopped loving you. If anything, I have stronger feelings for you now than I did, even, when you were a baby. I'll do anything I can to help you. But you have to be honest with me."

"She didn't want to do it," he said. "Pepper talked her into it."

"Pepper?"

"Her husband: His name is Francis, but everybody calls him Pepper. It's a nickname he grew up with."

"The policeman?"

"Ex-policeman." He paused. "He was thrown off the force three years ago."

"For being a jewel thief?"

"For accepting bribes." Steve threw a quick glance in my direction. "He got sort of, well, bent."

"I see. And since then?"

"Well, I guess he's been a crook. He was a crook before, too, I guess—that's why he got thrown off the force. But, well—he got mixed up with these friends of his, and he talked Georgette into helping him. She didn't want to."

I was going to ask him what means of persuasion Pepper had used but I decided I didn't have to—I could figure it out for myself. Money. "According to the man from the FBI," I said, "she has a very good eye."

"She's always liked jewelry," Steve admitted.

"So she helped Pepper and she got a cut, and you wear Gucci loafers."

"Jesus, what have you got against my shoes?"

I looked at him. He looked away.

"All right," he said. "I know." Then he forced himself to meet my gaze, and he smiled. "She gave them to me for my birthday." He took the shoes off. "Is that better?"

"Not really," I said. But I couldn't help smiling back at him.

"It was wrong, I suppose. I did have those jobs, though. I paid for all the groceries."

"Did you know what Georgette was doing?"

Another big question. But this one he answered promptly. "No. I just found out about it a couple of weeks ago, when the trouble started. I thought that with the money I was making and the money she was making—she was working in this beauty shop, see, in Beverly Hills—well, I thought that with that there were no problems. And then she said that Pepper was giving her money."

"Which he undoubtedly was. What kind of trouble started?"

"Some of the guys got caught."

"Oh."

"And now the cops are after Georgette. But it's not the cops we're afraid of. It's Pepper."

"Pepper didn't get caught?"

Steve shook his head.

"How come?"

"He wasn't there."

"I think you'd better explain."

He did. There were eight men in the gang. Not all of them participated in all the jobs. Four had been involved in this particular robbery. Two of the four had been caught, and two had got away. One of the two who'd been caught had been shot. He'd died of his wound but before dying he'd made a statement. The statement implicated Georgette.

"What about the other three?" I asked.

"Well, one is in jail. He's being held without bond. He won't talk, though. They're not worried about him. And the other two —I don't know where they are. Mexico, I think."

"And the four who didn't participate?"

"He didn't mention them."

"How do you know he didn't?"

"Pepper found out."

"Pepper found out? You mean he has contacts in the police department?"

Steve nodded.

"I'll be Goddamned."

"He knows that they're after Georgette. The police, I mean. They want to make a deal with her. If she'll tell them what she knows, if she'll testify, they won't prosecute her."

"And Pepper's afraid she'll make the deal."

"They're all afraid she'll make the deal. But Pepper's the one who's supposed to kill her."

"How do you know?"

"Because he already tried once."

9

I called Rita. I told her not to expect me for dinner.

"I know," she said. "Julie told me. What's he like?"

"Like me," I said. "All screwed up."

She laughed. Then she said, "I'm really happy for you, darling. I'm dying to meet him. Will you bring him over tomorrow?"

"I don't think tomorrow would be a very good day."

"What time are you supposed to check in at the hospital?"

"Afternoon. But if you'd like company for breakfast I'll bring myself over."

"I'd love company for breakfast. What about later tonight?"

"I don't think so, honey. I'm kind of tuckered out."

"I understand. Do you want to say good-bye to Julie? She's going back to Champaign in a little while."

"Sure."

Julie came on the line. I said good-bye to her. She said, "Your son is a doll."

"I know," I said.

Rita took over. She said that Terry had told her to say hi to me.

"Is he still there?" I asked.

"Naturally."

"I don't like that guy, Rita."

"I know you don't, darling. I'll see you tomorrow." She blew a kiss into the telephone and hung up.

I went back to Steve. He was again gazing out of the window. I joined him there.

"What are those little buildings?" he asked.

"The farm animals' zoo," I said.

"The park is nice with all the snow."

"I prefer it in the spring myself, and in the summer. The snow after a while gets kind of dirty."

He turned away from the window, found his glass and then found the bottle of Scotch. He applied the bottle to the glass. He still had his shoes off. "You must be sorry I turned up, being I'm in such a mess," he said.

"No, I'm not sorry you turned up," I said. "But I am worried. And I'd like to help in some way."

"You can't."

"I still can't believe that on the one hand Pepper warned his wife that she was in danger and on the other hand he tried to kill her."

"Why?"

"It doesn't make sense."

"Sure it does. Pepper's thinking about Pepper."

"I suppose." And, actually, the way Steve had told the story, it did fit together.

Georgette had received a telephone call at one o'clock in the morning. The call was from Pepper. Trouble, he said. Something had gone wrong. The police had caught Lou and Dave. Dave had been shot. She'd better get out of town for a while.

Georgette left immediately. With Steve. They went to a motel in San Bernardino. And there she told him the truth.

"Didn't that turn you off?" I asked.

"In a way," Steve admitted. "But—well—" He faltered.

I looked at him. I tried to understand.

"Well, she was in trouble. I couldn't just leave her."

"Couldn't, or didn't want to?"

He thought about that. "Both, maybe."

He and Georgette remained at the motel for a week. She was in touch with Pepper through his cousin. Pepper had left town also. He was in Pomona. It was the cousin who told her that the police were looking for her and wanted to make a deal. That Pepper thought she should take a long trip. That Pepper had five thousand dollars for her, to see her through the next few months.

Steve drove with Georgette to the cousin's house. The cousin wasn't there. Pepper was. Instead of five thousand dollars, he had a gun.

Steve threw an ashtray. The shot went wild. Steve lunged. The second shot went wild too—it grazed Georgette's thigh. The third shot went through the ceiling. Plaster fell, but that was all. There were no more shots. Pepper had hit his head on a table.

Yes, I thought, it did fit together. And Georgette was now caught between the law and Pepper. With Steve at her side.

"There's only one thing for you to do," I said. "Forget about Georgette. I'll take you to see Burr, and you can tell him everything you know."

Steve shook his head.

"Don't be an idiot," I said.

"She's been too nice to me. You yourself said—"

"Don't be an idiot."

"Besides, I'd never be able to prove that I wasn't mixed up in the thing too. They could get me as being an accessory or something."

"They aren't interested in you. They only want to know where Georgette is."

"You believe that?"

"Yes."

"Well, I don't."

"Steve, don't be an idiot."

"There's no way I could go to the FBI and tell them what I know and then not testify if they want me to."

I considered. He could be right about that.

"Suppose I do agree to testify. Pepper would kill me before I ever got on the stand."

"Pepper would be in jail."

"Then one of the others would."

"They'd be in jail too."

"Maybe not all of them."

"And if you told Burr where to find Georgette, would she talk?"

"I don't know. I don't think so. I think she'd be afraid."

There was a silence. Steve regarded the drink in his hand. He seemed to have changed his mind about it. He put it on the table. "Dad," he said finally. "I don't want anything to happen to Georgette."

It was as simple as that.

"The FBI would protect her," I said.

"Would they?"

For a while, I thought. Or perhaps not at all. Incriminating witnesses did have accidents. I said nothing.

"Let me handle this, Dad."

I studied him. Physically he appeared to be a man. But he'd only been out of high school for a year. And although he'd had some extraordinary experiences he still had plenty to learn. I sighed.

"Don't look at me like that."

"I can't help it."

Neither of us spoke for a while. Finally I asked him where he was staying.

"I think it's better if you don't know."

"Don't you trust me?"

"I just think it's better, that's all."

I didn't argue with him. "Do you trust me to buy you dinner?"

He grinned. "That I'll go along with."

"What about Georgette?"

"What about her?"

"Will she join us?"

"No. She still has a sore leg."

"I'll get my jacket," I said. I went into the bedroom. I felt terribly tired and was tempted to take my temperature again. I didn't, however. What good would it do me to know?

We went to Farber's for dinner and had rib-eye beef. During the meal the tired feeling got worse, and I began to sweat. I said nothing. Steve noticed, however. "You don't look so hot," he said.

"The drinks," I said. "Or maybe the surprise of seeing you."

"I didn't mean to upset you." There was concern in his voice.

Suppose he tries to get in touch with me while I'm in the hospital, I thought. "Actually, I have been a little under the weather. I'm going into the hospital tomorrow for a couple of days. Tests. Nothing serious."

His expression showed genuine anxiety. "Gee. I just found you and—"

"It's nothing to worry about," I assured him. I could feel the beads of moisture on my upper lip and on my forehead. "Really."

He didn't appear to be convinced.

"What did you think of Julie?" I asked.

"Affirmative," he replied. "Definitely affirmative. What does she do?"

"She goes to the University of Illinois, downstate."

"One of those, huh?" He didn't sound disapproving. But he did sound condescending.

"You don't like college girls?"

"Some of them are all right. But some of them have led such sheltered lives."

And you haven't? I thought. "I'll be home again the middle of the week," I said. "Will you come to see me?"

"Sure," he said, I detected a certain affection in his eyes. "You know I will." He paused. "You worry me, though. You don't look like you've been taking very good care of yourself."

"I'll be much better in a few days. You're the one who has to be careful."

"I'll be OK," he said. Then he smiled. "I'm glad we finally found each other. We almost didn't, you know."

I nodded. If Steve's reflexes had been a split second slower, or Pepper's a split second faster, Steve might have died a stranger to me. "Please be careful," I said.

He crossed his heart and raised his right hand.

10

"My goodness," Rita said. She appeared to have just got out of bed. "It's only nine o'clock."

"I couldn't sleep," I said.

She glanced at the zippered canvas bag in my hand. She said nothing. She simply drew me into her arms and kissed me. Then she said, "Tell me all about Steve. I want to hear everything."

We went into the living room. She'd evidently spent the evening housecleaning. The place looked the same now as it usually did on Friday nights. I plunked myself down in Walter's Chair and told her the whole story.

She was appalled. "We simply have to get him away from that woman," she said.

I wondered at her use of "we" but didn't comment. It had probably taken her no time at all to feel involved. If Steve was my son, then he was "our" problem. "That's easier said than done," I replied.

"Do you think he's that much in love with her?"

"I think he *was* that much in love with her. I doubt that he is now. What he feels now, in my opinion, is obligated to her. I'm not sure, though."

"But she's almost ten years older than he is, Walter."

"She doesn't look it. Would you like to see the picture again?" I had it in my pocket. I was taking it to the hospital with me.

"Yes."

We studied the picture together.

"You're right," Rita concluded. "She doesn't."

I put the picture away.

"But suppose he decides he wants to marry her," she said.

"How can he marry her? She's married to the ex-policeman. It's not divorce we're talking about. It's murder."

Rita shuddered. I guessed that she was recalling the time her husband had tried to murder her.

"In your case it was different," I said.

She nodded.

"No, I think I'll be able to bring him around," I said. "He'll eventually see the light. It may take a little time, though."

"He must be even better-looking than he is in the picture. Julie said he was handsome."

"He is. Like me. Now what about breakfast?"

Rita went into the kitchen. I tagged along. She fixed sausages and eggs and toasted bagels. We talked some more about Steve and Georgette and then about Julie and Terry. We agreed that you can't run your children's lives but that at times it's worth a try.

And at one-thirty I left. I took a taxi to the hospital. Rita wanted to go with me, but I dissuaded her. I also told her I hoped she wouldn't come to see me while I was there. She insisted that she would, though.

On Monday morning they gave me the first injection. Fenwick had explained that it would make me sick. But he hadn't explained that it would make me as sick as it did. I threw up for what seemed like an hour and felt terrible for the entire day.

55

I began to dread the next two injections.

Rita came in on her way home from the office. She brought me a book of crossword puzzles. She knew that I liked to work them. But she took one look at me and forgot about the book. "My goodness, Walter!" she exclaimed. "You're like a ghost. What kind of tests are they giving you?"

"The rabbit test," I said. "They think I may be pregnant."

"I mean it, darling."

"I'm OK. I'll be out in a couple of days."

"I don't like it."

"Sit down and tell me about your day. I'm sure that whatever it was like it was better than mine."

She did. It had been an average day. She couldn't make much of a story out of it. She appeared not to know whether to stay or leave. After a while I told her that she ought to leave. She still seemed undecided. I told her I was sleepy. She nodded and put on her coat. "I'll be back tomorrow," she promised.

"I wish you wouldn't, honey."

"Don't be silly."

I couldn't eat the dinner they brought me. I couldn't do any of the crossword puzzles either. I couldn't think of the simplest words. I began to get depressed. Really depressed.

To fight the depression I took a walk in the corridor. While walking I met the man who had the room next to mine. He was an old man. And, unfortunately, a sad old man. He wasn't altogether senile but he wasn't in full possession of his faculties either. He kept calling me Captain and telling me about a house that he had in Florida. From the way he talked I thought that he still owned the house, but it later developed that he didn't own it and never had—he'd rented it one winter, thirty years before. And whenever a nurse came by he leered and said, "Hello, sweetheart." He did nothing for my mood, and after a few minutes I retreated to my own room.

Depression is a strange thing. Most of what you think when you're depressed is true. You exaggerate it, that's all. My thoughts traveled along the same lines as on Saturday afternoon. I should have made something of my life but I hadn't, and now there wasn't going to be enough time. Somewhere I'd missed the boat, and it was too late to catch up with it. Why hadn't I been more successful? Was it lack of energy? Indifference? No, not lack of energy—as a young man I'd had enough energy for six people. I'd never really been indifferent either— if anything, I tried too hard. So what was it? In the three most important areas of a man's life—career, marriage, parenthood —I'd failed. Why?

And it was too late to make amends.

When the nurse asked me whether I wanted a sleeping pill I said yes.

The next morning they gave me the second injection. It made me as sick as the first had done.

In the course of his afternoon rounds Fenwick came into the room to see how I was getting along. I told him I was feeling terrible. He examined me. Although I might be feeling terrible, he said, I was responding well. The swelling had begun to go down, and I didn't have a fever. He patted me on the shoulder and said that he was encouraged.

My hopes rose. "You mean there may be a chance, after all?"

He gave me a smile. The sort of smile that's meant to inspire optimism but when it comes from a doctor seldom does. "Let's take one thing at a time," he said.

My hopes crashed.

"By this time next week you'll be feeling much better."

"How long will that last?"

He sat down on the side of the bed. "Walter, do you want me to lie to you?"

I really did. "No," I said.

"We went over it last week."

I gathered the courage to ask him what I'd been afraid to ask before. "When the end does come, Milton, what will it be like? Will it be bad?"

"Is that what's worrying you?"

"It's one of the things."

"It needn't."

I waited for him to go on. At first I thought he wasn't about to, but then he did.

"You'll have a short, overwhelming infection. Don't ask me what kind. It can be any kind. Pneumonia, an infection of the bloodstream—most likely an infection of the bloodstream. It won't last long, and you won't suffer." He looked at me. "That's the truth."

I nodded.

"Would you like me to give you some pills to put you in a better frame of mind?"

"Can you?"

"Yes."

"Then I'd like them. I've been feeling kind of low."

"I'll give you a prescription before you leave the hospital."

We made conversation for another few minutes, and he went out.

I wasn't alone for long, however. Shortly after four o'clock Burr arrived. With an enormous tabletop book on sports. The pictures were magnificent.

I was astonished. By the book and by the fact that he'd come. "How did you know where I am?" I asked.

"We always get our man. You know that."

I smiled.

"We got Dillinger, didn't we? And Baby-Face Nelson. And Dutch Schultz. And—would you like me to go on? Anyway, you were easier. The switchboard operator at the office handled it all by herself."

"It was really awfully nice of you, Ed."

He pointed to the book. "Look at page a hundred and one, why don't you?"

I looked at page a hundred and one. There was a picture of me. With the ball in my hand, running. "Well, I'll be damned!"

"Your senior year," Burr said.

I nodded. "Where did you find this thing?"

"I saw it in a bookstore a couple of months ago. It's new, for

Christmas. I was going to buy it for my wife to give me. You're the only one in the whole book that I ever met personally."

"Well, I'll be damned," I said again. I couldn't take my eyes off the picture. Steve resembled me more than I'd thought.

Burr sat down. "Remember the Stanford game that year?"

"Of course. I gained two hundred and thirty-six yards."

"Two hundred and sixty-three."

"Was it two hundred and sixty-three?"

"We clobbered them."

We reminisced about that game and others. It was pleasant. What made it pleasant weren't the memories themselves—many of the games had become blurred in my mind, and the Walter Jackson who'd gained two hundred and sixty-three yards against Stanford seemed an entirely separate individual from my present self. What made it pleasant was the expression on Burr's face. His eyes were shining. I'd never seen a man looking happier.

But at the same time I felt uneasy, and the longer Burr stayed, the more uneasy I became. There was practically no chance that Steve would come to the hospital. But then, I hadn't expected Burr either. And if Steve should come while Burr was there . . .

When the door opened, my heart skipped a beat.

It wasn't Steve, though. It was Rita. I tried to warn her with my eyes. I didn't think it was necessary—Rita had adequate presence of mind—but I wasn't sure.

I introduced them. They smiled at each other and shook hands.

"A pleasure," Burr said.

"Walter has told me about you," Rita said. "I've been hoping we'd meet."

I shot Burr a warning glance too. I didn't think he'd let any careless remarks drop either but I felt uneasy.

"We've been talking over old times," Burr said. "I was at Southern Cal when Walter was there. He was the best running back we'd ever had. I don't think there's been one like him since, for that matter. Show her the picture, Walter."

I explained about the book and showed Rita the picture.

If she had any thoughts about the resemblance between the picture of me and the picture of Steve she kept them to herself. "My goodness," she said. "You were handsome. But why did you have such an angry look on your face?"

"Because in the play before some guy had jabbed his knee into my stomach." It wasn't true, as far as I could recall, but it was the first explanation that occurred to me.

"Is that a fact?" Walter said. "Who?"

"I don't remember," I said. "It's too long to nurse a grudge."

Rita turned the page. Then she turned a few more pages. "It's a lovely book," she said.

"The wife and I would like you and Walter to come out to the house for dinner," Burr said. "One night next week, maybe."

"We'd love to," Rita told him, "but it all depends on how Walter's feeling." She glanced at me. There was anxiety in her eyes.

"Of course." There was anxiety in his eyes also.

"Walter'll be feeling fine," I said quickly. I wished that one of them would leave. Preferably Burr. "You'll be late for dinner," I suggested to him.

"The wife isn't expecting me," he replied. "We have a staff meeting tonight. I have to go back to the office."

"Does the FBI have staff meetings?" Rita asked.

"Sure," Burr said. "Everybody has staff meetings. And inter-office memos."

"But no bridal showers," Rita said.

Burr laughed. "Not recently."

I thought of some questions I'd like to ask him. In a round-about way. Concerning a man named Pepper Himes. I tried to figure out how I could. I decided I couldn't.

"Well," he said at last, "if I'm going to get anything to eat before the meeting starts I'd better be going." He put on his overcoat. "They're predicting more snow tonight. We're getting it early this year. Looks like a long winter."

He held out his hand. I took it.

"Take it easy, fellow," he said.

I thanked him again for the book. He left.

Rita waited a moment, then said in a low voice, "You didn't tell him about Steve, did you?"

I replied in a low voice that I hadn't.

11

What I'd been afraid would happen on Tuesday happened on Wednesday. Steve came to the hospital.

Burr wasn't there. Rita wasn't there. The only person who was in the room with me was a nurse. She was wiping my face. I'd just vomited.

Steve immediately became alarmed. "Jeez, you're really sick!"

I made an effort to pull myself together. "No," I said.

"You are," he insisted.

"Tell him I'm not sick," I instructed the nurse.

"He's not sick," she said.

Steve didn't look convinced.

The nurse finished her chores and left.

"I'm worried about you," Steve said.

I took a deep breath. "Don't," I said. Another deep breath. "I'm going home this afternoon." It was true. Fenwick had already made the arrangements.

"Are you sure you should?"

"Yes. I'm OK."

"Well," he said dubiously.

"Really," I assured him.

He brightened. "I changed my shoes." He held one of his feet up, to show me.

I smiled. "How did you know where to find me?"

"I just kept calling hospitals."

"How's Georgette?"

"Pretty good." He noticed the book on the dresser. "What's that?"

"A sports book. There's a picture of me in it."

"No kidding?" He picked up the book and began turning the pages. "Where?"

"Somewhere. I don't remember the page."

He kept turning the pages until he found it. "Holy smoke!" He studied the picture for quite a while. "Jeez, this is nice!" He looked at some of the other pictures but came back to the one of me. "Holy smoke!"

I got out of bed and put on my robe. The room swam for a few seconds, but then I got my balance. I went over to Steve and viewed the picture over his shoulder. "You look a lot like I did at that age."

"You think so?" He sounded pleased. "In a way I do, I guess." He finally closed the book. He continued to hold it, however. "Where did you get this thing?"

"A friend gave it to me." I hesitated. There was no reason to keep it a secret. "The FBI man I was telling you about."

He quickly put the book on the bed and surveyed the room, as if the FBI man might be hiding someplace. "I didn't know you and he were so buddy-buddy."

"Neither did I. He's a nice fellow, though."

Steve gave me a questioning look.

"I didn't tell him about you," I said.

He heaved a sigh. "Did he say anything more about Georgette?"

"No." Rita was right, I thought: we had to get him away from that woman. "I'd like to meet Georgette," I said.

His expression became suspicious. "Why?"

"Because she's part of your life and you're part of my life."

He thought about that for a while. "I suppose." The suspicious look disappeared. "You're liable to like her, you know."

"I don't expect not to like her."

"I'll see what I can work out. You'll be home tonight?"

"Tonight and for the next few nights. Unless I'm at Mrs. Swift's. I'll give you her telephone number, in case."

"OK."

I gave him Rita's number. I was going to give him mine too, but he said he already had it—the way he'd found me in the first place was through looking in the telephone directory. He said he'd be in touch with me—unless I wanted him to stick around and drive me home. I told him that that wouldn't be necessary —Mrs. Swift was going to pick me up. Which was true. She was taking the afternoon off, against my wishes, and had arranged for Terry to drive us, also against my wishes.

Steve picked up the book again, held it for a moment, then put it down, said he'd be seeing me and left.

I went back to bed.

Terry was more subdued than usual. He was wearing jeans and a Navy peacoat, and his hair, which was usually in carefully arranged disorder with a lot of spray on it, was neat. Instead of calling me Wally, as was his habit, he called me Mr. Jackson, and instead of chattering, as he usually did, he had little to say.

In fact, none of us had much to say. I sat in the front seat with Terry, and Rita sat in the back, holding a large bag of groceries, to keep it from falling over. She'd had Terry stop at the Jewel on the way to the hospital, and she'd laid in a supply of extras she thought I needed. She was planning, she said, to fix dinner for the two of us at my apartment.

Driving was difficult. More snow had fallen during the night. The thoroughfares had been cleared, but most of the side streets hadn't, and the pavement was slippery. I kept glancing at Terry and waiting for him to speak, but he didn't. He didn't even turn his head; he seemed to be entirely concerned with getting us safely over the three miles from the hospital to the building I lived in.

Finally I said, "It was nice of you to come and get me, Terry."

" 'Snothing," he replied, and lapsed into silence again.

But then when we were a block from our destination he cracked. He revealed what was on his mind. "Your son," he said, "where does he go to school?"

"He doesn't," I said.

"He must have a good job, then."

"Um."

"That jacket he had on—" Terry didn't finish the sentence. He didn't have to, though. I suddenly understood what was bothering him. Julie had expressed a favorable opinion of Steve. Terry was feeling challenged.

The conversation went no further, and we arrived at my building in three-way gloom. Terry offered to carry the groceries up to the apartment, but Rita said it wasn't necessary, and he drove off.

The apartment looked good to me. I tossed my overcoat across a chair. "God, it's a pleasure to be back."

"I can imagine." Rita took the groceries into the kitchen.

I walked into the bedroom. I noticed the thermometer on the table and quickly put it away. I could hear Rita moving back and forth in the kitchen, cabinet doors opening and closing.

"Do you want a drink?" Rita called.

A drink was the one thing I didn't want. "A Coke, maybe," I called back.

There were sounds of rummaging. "You haven't got any," Rita reported. "Just tonic."

"Tonic'll do."

I went back to the living room. Rita joined me, bringing two tall glasses of tonic. She'd put a maraschino cherry in each. I smiled. "Those cherries have been there for months."

"They don't spoil. Well, here's to no more tests."

"I'll drink to that."

"What did Fenwick say?"

"Pressure on a nerve." I thought of the prescription he'd given me to improve my state of mind. It was in my pocket, along with the receipt from the hospital. "He gave me something to take."

"You ought to take it."

"I will. But first I have to have it filled."

"Give it to me. I'll take it down to the drugstore."

"There's no hurry." I removed the prescription from my pocket. Also the receipt. I put them on the desk. Then I stood there for a moment. Something was wrong.

"What's the matter?" Rita asked.

I continued to stand there. I'd left some letters on the desk, along with the form for my state income tax. The letters had been on top of the form. Someone had moved them. And the top page of the form was torn. The tear wasn't a large one, but I was quite certain it hadn't been there before. "Were you in the apartment while I was in the hospital?" I asked.

"No."

I opened the desk drawers, one at a time. Nothing was where it should have been. I turned to Rita. "Well, someone was."

"What do you mean?" She came over to me.

I explained.

Together we went through the drawers of the dresser in the bedroom and through the closets. Nothing, as far as I could determine, had been stolen. But certain items had been moved around.

"I don't understand it," Rita said.

"Neither do I. You're the only one besides me who has a key."

"It wasn't me. What about the manager of the building?"

"She has a passkey to all the apartments."

"Then it was probably her."

"I've known her for years. She wouldn't go through my things."

"You'd better ask her."

I did. Her name was Mrs. Moriarity. She had an apartment on the second floor. She assured me that she hadn't been in my unit, as she called it, and that she hadn't given her key to anyone else either. She kept the keys on numbered hooks in a cabinet, and the cabinet was locked. Just to make certain, however, she opened the cabinet while Rita and I watched her. The key to my apartment was in its usual place.

"I'm sorry to have troubled you," I said, and Rita and I went back upstairs.

"Could it have been Steve?" Rita asked.

"I very much doubt it," I said. "He doesn't have a key, and there's nothing here that would interest him particularly."

"Who, then?"

"I don't know." I began to have a funny feeling, though. It started at the back of my neck and traveled down my spine.

An ex-policeman, I thought, might have all kinds of keys.

12

Steve called at nine. He'd talked to Georgette. She wouldn't mind meeting me. I invited the two of them for dinner the next evening. Dinner would be all right, Steve said, if I could find some nice quiet place. He emphasized quiet. I said that that was no problem. I named a German restaurant on the northwest side and told him where it was.

I invited Rita to join us. She agreed readily.

Rita spent the night. She fixed breakfast, then went to work.

I sat around, thinking. I came to the conclusion that Steve and Georgette were in no more danger in Chicago than they would be anyplace else. They'd be in danger wherever they went.

I decided that I needed help, though, and that Burr was the one to give it to me. The kind of help I needed would be no problem for him. Information. I wondered whether I could get the information without revealing anything myself. It seemed to me that I could.

So I dug out the card he'd given me and got ready to go

downtown. My car hadn't been out of the garage since Saturday, and I had plans for it, so I drove it into a gas station, bought gas, had the tires and battery checked, then went to the FBI office.

Burr was out. The receptionist didn't know when he'd be back but she thought that he might be gone for the rest of the day. I was disappointed. I should have called, I thought. I'd made a trip for nothing.

Then I remembered Charly. I walked over to the Insurance Exchange Building and went up to my office. I looked out of the window. Charly's light was on. He was using the telephone. I hung up my coat and went around to the Kipness spread.

"It was those two moving violations," Charly was explaining. "Plus the neighborhood you live in. That's what makes it so high. . . . Yes, I agree, but unfortunately any other company would charge at least that much." He saw me and motioned for me to sit down.

I did, and waited for him to finish his call.

He had a hard time finishing it. I gathered from what I was hearing at my end that he was attempting to explain to a client why the premium for his auto insurance was as much as it was and that he *had* shopped around—this was the best he could do.

He went through the motions of mopping his brow, for my benefit, and made a face at the telephone, also for my benefit. He finally succeeded in bringing the conversation to a close.

"The poor kid," he said after he hung up. "Six hundred and thirty-one dollars for a Mustang."

"How old a kid?"

"Nineteen. With two moving violations and one minor accident in the past twelve months."

I nodded. I knew.

"Where've you been all week?" Charly asked. "Your place has been dark."

"Goofing off," I told him.

"What kind of goofing off can you do in this kind of weather?"

His kind of goofing off was golf. Any other kind of goofing off he didn't understand as well. Golf and handball. He belonged to the Y.

I shrugged. "Feel like lunch?"

"Why not?"

We went to one of the restaurants in the building, and over lunch I sized him up more carefully than I'd ever done before. He wasn't a bad human being. Or a bad insurance man. What he lacked was drive. He'd probably had it at some point in the past but had become discouraged. He'd decided to settle for what he had. But he wasn't without a sense of responsibility.

"I've been thinking," I said. "I've about made up my mind to go back to California."

His eyes widened. "Isn't this kind of sudden?"

"Yes and no. I've really been thinking about it for quite a while. The thing is, if I do, I'd like to turn my business over to you."

"You mean Carling-Small?" His voice cracked.

"I don't know about Carling-Small. Ben might give that to someone else. But all the other stuff."

"Would you want a piece of it?"

"No, Charly, I wouldn't."

He eyed me from several angles, with different expressions.

"There's no catch," I said.

"God, Walter!"

"We'll talk about it some more, but in the meanwhile I thought I'd let you know."

We went back to his office, then I went to my own. There was an accumulation of mail. I opened it, sorted it and wrote some letters to give to the public stenographer to type for me. I also forwarded a claims form which had been sent to me by Mrs. Robinson, whose fur coat had been stolen.

The public stenographer said she'd have the letters ready for me to sign the next morning. I went from her office to the FBI. Burr had called in, the receptionist said; he wouldn't be back for the balance of the day. But why didn't I leave my name? I left it.

I started for the garage where my car was. After walking for half a block, however, I decided that I didn't want to go home and sit around, that it would be better simply to walk. I turned around and started east on Jackson. The air felt good. It was cold, but there was no wind. At Michigan Avenue I turned north and presently found that I was retracing the steps I'd taken at the same time of day, exactly one week before. I retraced them all the way to the bar at the Wrigley Building.

The bartender recognized me. He smiled and said, "Good afternoon."

The place was quiet but not as quiet as it had been the last time. There were a few holdovers from the lunch hour.

"Martini?" the bartender said.

"OK," I said, simply because he had a good memory.

One of the holdovers was the man who'd been there before. At first I couldn't recall his name, but then it came to me. Franken. He was with someone else this time. Both of them were drunk, but Franken was the drunker of the two. He had his elbow on the bar and was supporting his head with his hand. It appeared to me that if his elbow slipped his head would go crashing onto the counter.

"So what I keep shaying, Garrishon, ish a man with your talent, with your quirky viewpoint, Garrishon, a man like you is wayshted with Robbins and Asher. I know."

"Quirky viewpoint," Garrison repeated, as if he liked the sound of the words. "Quirky viewpoint."

"Quirky viewpoint," Franken assured him.

I eavesdropped as I sipped my drink. I wondered what had happened to the poor slob whose layout Franken hadn't liked. I also wondered why Franken had allowed himself to get drunk with a man he was trying to hire. I decided that he was having trouble with one of his accounts. Probably one of the big accounts. The pressure was getting to be too much for him, and

Garrison was his last hope. Garrison with his quirky viewpoint.

They were still talking when I left. Neither was making much sense.

I took a cab back to the garage and drove home.

The telephone was ringing when I got there. I could hear it from the corridor outside the apartment. Burr, I thought—and hurried to unlock the door.

I grabbed the telephone on the sixth ring and said, "Hello."

There was a click at the other end of the line. Then nothing. I sighed and put the telephone back on its cradle. I hung up my coat. It would be difficult to get anything from Burr over the telephone; I needed to see him in person. All I could do over the telephone would be to make a date. But that was better than nothing.

I called the FBI office. Mr. Burr hadn't returned, the switchboard operator informed me. He hadn't called in again either. She hadn't given him my name. Couldn't someone else help me? No, I said, and hung up.

Ten minutes later the doorbell rang. I pushed the button to unlock the downstairs door, opened the door of my apartment and waited.

The man who stepped out of the automatic elevator was a stranger to me. He was a big man. He was wearing a tan raincoat and he looked cold.

"Mr. Jackson?" he said.

I nodded.

"My name is Wentworth. I wonder if I can speak to you for a few minutes." He reached into his pocket and took out a business card, which he gave me.

The card said that he was Ralph Wentworth. Under his name was the name of a company—Farr and Driscoll, Private Investigators, Established 1923.

"What do you want?" I said.

"To ask you a few questions." He rubbed his hands together, to warm them. "May I come in?"

I stepped aside and followed him into the apartment. He

didn't take off his coat. I looked at the card again and put it in my own pocket. He chose a chair and sat down, planting his feet firmly but keeping his spine straight.

"Terrible weather," he said. "I'm glad I don't have to live here."

"Where do you live?" I asked.

"Los Angeles."

I considered him, a little at a time. Not quite as tall as I was, but tall. About thirty-five, with prematurely graying hair. Nice features. Big hands. Big feet, too. But either he was anemic or he was half frozen—his skin was very pale. And there was no trace of a sense of humor in his eyes.

"What questions do you have?" I asked.

"I'm working on an inquiry about your son, Mr. Jackson."

"An inquiry?"

"You might call it that. I'm trying to locate him."

"I see."

"I'm at liberty to tell you who my client is. There's nothing secret about it. I'm working on behalf of his parents, Mr. and Mrs. Delmore Livingston of Bel-Air, California. They haven't seen their son or heard from him in a number of months and they're worried. They've hired my company to trace him."

"I see. How did you get my name?"

"Mr. and Mrs. Livingston supplied it. Among others."

"I haven't seen him. Not in seven years. And it isn't likely that I will."

He regarded me with a steady gaze.

"Who are some of the other names on the list?" I asked.

"That, I'm afraid, is confidential." He blew on his hands, without taking his eyes off me.

"You ought to get yourself a pair of gloves," I said.

"Has Steve Livingston called you or written to you, Mr. Jackson?"

"Not in seven years. And there's little chance that he will. He doesn't like me very much. Mr. and Mrs. Livingston saw to that."

"Then you don't know where he is?"

"I do not."

He hesitated, still studying me, then got up. "Well, thank you very much, Mr. Jackson. I appreciate your time."

I saw him out. As soon as the elevator door closed I took the card out of my pocket. Established 1923, but no address or telephone number.

I went into the bedroom and dialed Los Angeles Information.

There was no listing for a Farr and Driscoll detective agency in Los Angeles.

I hung up. That doesn't mean there can't be a Farr and Driscoll detective agency somewhere else, I reminded myself.

But somehow I didn't believe that there was.

13

Rita and I got to the restaurant first. I gave my name to the headwaiter, and we went to the bar. The bartender looked like a small Hermann Goering. In lederhosen, yet.

We sat down next to a couple who might have been Willy Brandt and Maria Schell but weren't. They were talking German, though.

"Beer?" I said to Rita.

She nodded. We'd been there a couple of times before; the beer was good. Rita's eyes were bright, the way they got when she was excited.

I ordered two beers. The bartender brought them. Large steins, with foam running down the sides.

The decor was ersatz Bavarian, with big, heavily decorated mugs on shelves and cuckoo clocks and a large oil painting of a buxom woman in something white that you could see through, reclining under a tree, with a deer nibbling grass at her feet. The waitresses were bustling around in dirndls and peasant blouses. All of the busboys had blond hair and pink cheeks, except for one who was Puerto Rican.

The clientele was authentic German-American or American-German—it was hard to tell at times which came first. Solid, conscientious citizens with abundant energy and big appetites.

"We ought to come here more often," I said.

"We ought," Rita agreed.

I said nothing about the detective named Wentworth. But I did say, "When they leave I'm going to follow them."

Rita withheld comment.

"I've got to find out where they're staying. Steve won't tell me."

She withheld comment on that also.

And before I could get further into the subject Steve appeared in the doorway. With Georgette. I waved. They came over.

Steve and I did the introducing. He eyed Rita. I did the same to Georgette.

Georgette was more beautiful, even, than she appeared in the photograph. Beautiful enough to make half the men in the room turn around to inspect her.

"You sure know how to pick 'em," I told Steve.

He grinned. Georgette smiled.

"Steve tells me you were a football player," she said.

"For a while," I admitted.

"I love football," she said.

I got the attention of the headwaiter, and he led us to a table. The previous party had just left, and the Puerto Rican busboy was setting it up. I recommended the beer to Steve and Georgette, and they ordered some. We got settled.

"I used to go to all the Rams games," Georgette said.

"Did you, now?" I replied.

I wasn't expecting the topic to go anyplace, but it did. Georgette evidently hadn't only gone to all the Rams games; she had an understanding of the mechanics of football that was greater than that of any woman I'd ever met. I was astonished. She had an interest in other sports, too, primarily tennis and swimming.

76

She'd grown up near the water, she said. She didn't say which body of water, but I suspected that she came from somewhere along the California coast, if not Los Angeles itself. I also suspected that if she and Steve had gone surfing together it was more because she liked to surf than because he did.

After a while the conversation swung the other way—in a Georgette-Rita direction. I took it easy and listened. Georgette was equally comfortable with such topics as food and furniture. She made it sound as if she was a good cook.

I tried to analyze her. I found it hard to do. She was certainly bright. Whether her knowledge of all the things she spoke about was deep or superficial I couldn't determine, but her knowledge of football certainly seemed to be deep. I guessed that she was one of those people who pick things up quickly, almost by osmosis. Also that somewhere, early in her life, she'd learned the importance of winning the approval of both men and women.

Steve seemed content to do what I was doing—sitting back and listening. With full confidence in Georgette's ability to handle herself. Confidence which was entirely justified.

Georgette didn't have much to say directly to him, though. She mentioned his name in connection with certain things they'd done together, places they'd been, and when she did it was in the tone of voice a woman might use when referring to a husband she'd been married to for years. Not without interest but without excitement. She was concentrating on Rita and me. As if she already had Steve and knew it and was now making an attempt to win us.

It was almost impossible to believe that she was mixed up with a ring of jewel thieves. Or even that she'd knocked about as much as she had.

Rita led the talk around to the recent past, then asked, "How did you two happen to come to Chicago?"

"We wanted to get away for a while," Georgette replied easily. "You have no idea how tiresome it can get, having the same weather all the time."

I'd never got tired of it, I thought. But I said nothing.

"Do you have friends or family here?" Rita asked.

"A girlfriend," Georgette replied, just as easily. "She used to be my best friend, but then she married a man from Chicago and moved here."

"Perhaps I know her," Rita suggested.

"I doubt it," Georgette replied with a smile.

The part about the girlfriend could be true, I thought. "North side?" I asked.

"Suburbs," Georgette replied.

I weighed the matter of telling them about the man who claimed to be a private investigator. It might shake some information loose. But it might also drive them right out of town. There would be no advantage to that, I decided. Anyone who could find them in Chicago could find them elsewhere—and I might lose them myself.

"I'm pretty well acquainted out in the suburbs," I said. "I have clients there."

No dice. Georgette gave me a dazzling smile and said, "I'm sure you must."

"The Chicago suburbs are pretty," Steve said.

"Have you been sightseeing without me?" Georgette quickly asked him.

Rita gave me a significant glance. Did you get that? it said.

I had. He'd seen the suburbs. So evidently the part about the girlfriend was true.

Steve picked up his cue. "A little," he said.

"They're even prettier in the spring," I said, and wondered if he'd told her how much I knew. There was nothing to indicate that he had.

The waitress cleared away the dinner plates. There were three kinds of dessert, she said: apple strudel, cherry strudel and cheese strudel. We discussed it and decided to try them all —two apple, one cherry, one cheese. The waitress left.

Over dessert and coffee Rita did a little more probing. She didn't get anywhere with it. Finally she gave up. We ended the

78

meal talking about the Donald Sutherland movie Rita and I had seen. Georgette too liked Donald Sutherland, she said.

Georgette kissed me on the cheek when we parted, and told Rita she'd loved meeting her. Anyone who liked Biedermeier furniture, she added, had to be A-OK.

Then the hard work started. Following Steve's car.

It's tough enough to follow a car through traffic when you have a general idea as to where you're going. It's much tougher when you don't. The only thing that worked in my favor was the fact that the streets were slippery and Steve couldn't go more than thirty-five miles an hour. That, and having four eyes instead of two. Whenever I lost sight of the car Rita knew where it was, and when she didn't see it I did.

I'd thought that the car might have California plates, but it didn't. It had no plates at all. Evidently it was newly purchased. And it was so dark in color that I couldn't tell whether it was blue or black.

The dark color made the car that much harder to tail. Twice I almost lost it. Once when Steve went through a yellow light, and once when he connected with a turn arrow and I missed it. Both times I caught up with him, however.

The route took us north and west from the restaurant, with a considerable amount of zigzagging. At first I was afraid that Steve was zigzagging because he knew he was being followed, but after a while it became apparent that this wasn't the reason. He simply didn't know his way around the city and couldn't find the thoroughfare he was looking for.

Eventually he found it, though. Lincoln Avenue. I could have told him how to get there, I thought, with a lot less trouble. Once he got onto it, he went in a straight line, and following him became easier. He and Georgette were staying with the girlfriend, I decided, and the girlfriend probably lived in Skokie.

Wrong.

They were staying at the Riverview Inn, within the city limits. A medium-sized, medium-priced motel, one of a cluster that had sprung up on Lincoln Avenue a number of years back, for no particular reason.

Steve turned into the parking lot so suddenly that I couldn't stop without skidding. I went past the place, made an illegal U-turn and came back.

The building was a two-story yellow brick structure, shaped like an L. The parking lot was on the inside of the L. I pulled up in front of the office and jumped out of the car. They wouldn't be registered under their real names, I thought. The only way to learn the number of their room was to trail them to the door.

I saw a pair of headlights go off at the far end of the parking area. I moved cautiously along the side of the building, under the overhang of the second-story balcony. I heard the car doors slam. I stopped and waited. The parking area wasn't well lit, but the sidewalk under the balcony was. Two figures emerged into the light and turned toward me. I flattened myself against the wall and pretended to be fumbling for a key. I held my breath.

The figures were Steve and Georgette. But after walking only a few yards toward me they stopped and turned into a recessed stairway. I hurried toward it. They were already out of sight when I got there. I climbed the steps on tiptoe. The steps ended at an open passageway that led out to the balcony. I peered around the corner. Steve was standing directly under a light. He was unlocking a door on the long side of the L. Georgette was standing behind him.

He got the door open, and they went inside.

I walked along the balcony and stopped at the window. The drapes were drawn. I continued to the door. The room number was two-eleven. While I was looking at it the television set inside the room went on.

I quickly moved away, descended the steps and went back to my car. Although the air was cold I was sweating.

"Room two-eleven," I said.

Rita said nothing.

I threw the gear into Drive and eased the car away from the

curb. No pressure now. I could relax.

We drove for perhaps a mile without speaking. Finally I said, "Well, what do you think of Georgette Himes?"

Rita summed it up very neatly. "That's the smoothest article I've ever met in my entire life," she said.

14

I dropped her off at her apartment and went back to mine. I sat up for a while, drinking tonic and watching the Late Show. The Late Show was about men from another planet who were going to destroy Earth. The planet they were from was named Pluton, and they had this radioactive substance called Borium. Or maybe it was the other way around and the radioactive substance was called Pluton. I couldn't concentrate.

The evening, it seemed to me, had been a waste. I'd met Georgette and learned where she and Steve were staying. I hadn't accomplished anything else, though. I hadn't even figured out what it would be possible to accomplish. It would be simple to turn Georgette over to the FBI. But if Steve ever found out I'd done that I'd lose him for the rest of my life.

The rest of my life? The words had a different meaning now.

If by losing him I'd be saving him it would be worth doing. I wouldn't necessarily be saving him, though. Pepper Himes was probably as eager to eliminate the threat from Steve as he was to eliminate the threat from his wife. He had to be smart enough to know that Steve at least had *some* information. Furthermore, Steve had been a witness to the attempted murder. Only when Pepper and every one of his associates were behind bars would Steve be safe.

I couldn't bring that about. No way. All I could do was get Steve out of the line of fire. By separating him from Georgette. And I didn't see how I could bring that about either.

In the middle of the battle scene I fell asleep. The Earth men, in one space ship, were firing rockets at the men from the other planet, who were in another space ship, and I don't know what happened after that.

At two o'clock I woke up and went to bed. I fell asleep again almost immediately.

When I woke the second time it was eight o'clock in the morning and the telephone was ringing.

It was Burr. He'd got my message. How was I feeling?

Fine, I said. I'd like to talk to him. Could I come to the office later in the day?

Unfortunately, no. He was calling me from the airport. He was on his way to Springfield, Illinois. Something important had come up.

In Springfield?

In Springfield. He'd be back tonight, though. He'd talked to his wife. How about dinner on Monday night?

Monday night would be fine, I said.

He said he had to run—they were announcing his flight. He hung up.

I stretched and went to the window. The sky was bright. The sun was actually shining. And Lincoln Park did look pretty with the snow on the trees. It really did.

Furthermore, I discovered, I wasn't feeling my usual self. I was feeling better. For the first time in what seemed like an eternity I felt quite well. It made a vast difference.

I shaved and showered. I shampooed my hair and clipped my toenails. I assembled the laundry that had accumulated during the past two weeks, took the pins out of a new shirt and prepared to meet the world with a smile.

It struck me that I could do something about Steve and Georgette after all. I might not be able to get him away from her, but there was a chance that I could get her away from him.

I went out for breakfast. To a little place that I sometimes stopped at, on Clark Street. I thought the matter over as I ate.

I had a chance. If logic wouldn't work, money might. What I had to do was talk to Georgette alone.

First get Georgette away from Steve, then get Steve away from everything. Once I'd accomplished stage one, Ben Small might be able to help me with stage two. Ben was entitled to my confidence anyway.

Putting the cart before the horse, I called Ben's office. I spoke with Nancy Morris, his secretary. We were telephone friends from way back. She was as nice a person as he was. We chatted. She told me that Ben was in Palm Beach for a couple of weeks. He was coming to Chicago a week from Friday for a meeting, then going to Washington for a few days, and from Washington he was going to Tokyo. She spoke to him at least twice a day, however, and she'd tell him that I'd called. He'd be pleased. He'd mentioned me to her not long ago.

I was disappointed but not surprised. And not too disappointed either. If necessary, I could go to Palm Beach.

I glanced at my watch. Nine-thirty. Too early to go to the motel. It was a nice day. I hadn't taken a walk in the park in months.

I walked for an hour. Through the zoo, past the flower conservatory, around the lagoon, up to Diversey and back. I stopped for a few minutes to see how the baby elephant was getting along. She'd been born the year before, and her birth had been duly reported in the newspapers and on television. It had been touch and go with the mother for a while, but now everything was all right. The baby was named Rosalie, and I was pleased to note that she was doing well. She was about five feet high, a placid creature. For a few moments she watched me watching her, then went on with what she'd been doing—

brushing the hay from her feet with her trunk. Everything else being equal, I thought, when everyone now alive on earth was dead and buried Rosalie would still be going strong.

There were a few people thawing out in the steamy heat of the flower conservatory, and some hardier souls were ice-skating on the lagoon, but for the most part the park was deserted. The limbs of the trees were bent under the weight of a layer of snow, and the ground was untrammeled white. The clarity of the air gave sharp definition to every surface and made each twig seem important. Looking around, I was filled with a strange ache. It wasn't physical but it was strong enough to seem physical. The world was so much more beautiful than I'd ever given it credit for being. It offered so much to enjoy and admire. Even this city—I'd never fully appreciated it. It had been a haven for me at a time when I needed one, and it had offered me the love of a woman at a time when I needed that too, and I'd felt grateful to it. But I'd never thought of it as being particularly attractive. It was, though. I hadn't seen most of the world, and now I never would, but I doubted that there were many cities that could match Chicago's lakefront and parks.

I walked slowly back to my starting point and got the car out of the garage. I drove to the Riverview Inn.

I left the car in front of the building, near the office, and walked through the parking lot. I went to the spot where Steve had left his car the night before. His car wasn't there. Most of the guests had either checked out or were gone for the day. Of the few cars left, none was without license plates. If that meant that Steve was out and Georgette was in, I was lucky. If it meant that both of them were out, I'd simply have to wait. The wait might be a long one.

I crossed the parking lot to the sidewalk under the overhang and found the stairway. I climbed the steps and went out onto the balcony. Some distance away, on the short leg of the L, a chambermaid with a heavy sweater over her uniform was pushing a cart of linens from one room to the next. I walked along the balcony to two-eleven, hoping that the drapes would be open wide enough for me to peer inside.

They weren't.

I hesitated. Suppose Georgette had taken the car and Steve was in the room. It might be a good idea to telephone first. But if I telephoned and Steve answered, what would I say? Or even if Georgette answered, what would I say?

I couldn't make up my mind. Perhaps I was trying to be too clever. Perhaps the thing to do was simply walk in on both of them and tell them what I thought.

I started to leave. I took two steps toward the stairway and stopped.

You came, I told myself. You had a purpose. See it through.

I went back to the door, raised my hand to knock, hesitated one last time, then rapped lightly.

There was no answer.

I waited a moment and rapped louder.

Still no answer.

I tried the knob. To my surprise, the door was unlocked. I opened it.

Steve wasn't there. Georgette was. She was sitting on the floor, her head resting against a chair at an awkward angle. Part of her face had been shot away.

15

I don't know how long I stood there. It was probably no more than a few seconds but it seemed much longer. I was too paralyzed to move even my eyes. I just stood perfectly still and stared at the ragged red pulp which had been the left side of a beautiful woman's face. Then my gorge began to rise, and that brought me into motion. I backed away, swallowing my own bile. Backed slowly out onto the balcony, trembling. Closed the door and wiped the knob with my overcoat. Moved unsteadily to the stairs. Took several deep breaths. Descended to the ground floor. Took another deep breath. And ran to my car.

I drove almost a mile before my brain unlocked. I found that I was going southeast on Lincoln Avenue, in the general direction of home. I continued in that direction, but not because of any conscious plan. I had no conception of what I'd do when I got home.

There was only one thing that mattered. I had to find Steve. Before the police did.

I parked the car in its assigned stall. I rang for the automatic elevator and when it came got in. I pushed the button for my floor, but the elevator stopped at two, and Mrs. Moriarity got in with me. The incinerator was blocked on the fourth floor, she reported, and she was going to investigate.

I nodded.

"Did you ever find out who got into your unit?" she asked.

I shook my head. "I must have been mistaken," I said in a tight voice.

She smiled as if glad to be vindicated and got out. I continued to the fifth floor and went into my apartment. I was still seeing Georgette's shattered face.

Before taking off my overcoat I poured myself three ounces of Scotch and gulped it. And before I could put the glass down the telephone rang.

"Where've you been?" Rita wanted to know. "I've been calling for the past two hours. You weren't at your office either."

"I was out." My voice was beginning to sound better.

"I know you were." Then she seemed to have an inkling. "Oh. Anything happen?"

"Nugh," I said.

"I can't understand you."

"I'll explain later."

"What time will you be over?"

"Be over? I don't know."

"Would you rather I came to your place tonight? There's plenty of food left."

"No. Yes. I don't know. I'll let you know later."

"Are you all right, darling?"

"I'm fine. I'll call you later. Don't worry." I hung up and poured myself another ounce of Scotch. Then I took off my overcoat.

I paced the floor. I smoked. I tried first one chair, then another. I went into the bedroom and lay down. I got up again and paced some more.

Steve didn't come. Steve didn't call.

At two o'clock I turned on the radio. There was plenty of

news. Nothing about Georgette, however.

I continued to chain-smoke and to move restlessly between the living room and the bedroom. I wanted to go out, if only to clear my head, but I was afraid that Steve might try to get in touch with me during my absence.

There was nothing about Georgette on the two-thirty news either.

But at three o'clock there was.

Police were investigating the slaying of a Mrs. Stanley Langston of Los Angeles, who was found shot to death early this afternoon in her room at the Riverview Inn on the city's northwest side. They were seeking the identity of a man in a plaid overcoat who was seen leaving Mrs. Langston's room shortly before noon.

I turned off the radio and sank down on the sofa.

I'd been wearing a plaid overcoat.

16

Time didn't pass any more quickly after the news than it had before. Nor did I have any better idea as to what to do.

The chambermaid must have been the one who described me. I tried to estimate the distance from where she'd been to where I'd been. Forty or fifty yards at least. She couldn't have seen me too well. Her description wouldn't have been very specific.

I went over in my mind the seconds I'd spent in the room. I was quite certain that I hadn't touched anything except the knob on the outside of the door, which I'd wiped.

It was possible that if the police questioned enough people they'd find someone who'd seen me running to my car and that that person had got a better look at me. But it was also possible that they wouldn't.

Meanwhile the only thing I could do other than go to the police and attempt to clear myself was buy a new overcoat.

Clearing myself would be a tough job. The police would want to know why I hadn't reported the murder immediately.

They'd also want to know what I was doing at the motel in the first place. Eventually I might be able to convince them that I wasn't the killer, but it would take time. And I wouldn't be able to do it without telling them everything I knew about Steve and his relationship with Georgette.

Where was Steve? Had Pepper Himes found him too? I tried to persuade myself that this wasn't the case. But if Pepper hadn't found him, the police would. Perhaps the police already had. What would he tell them? What *could* he tell them?

Where was he?

Steve would have an even harder time establishing his innocence than I would. I could imagine the questions. What is your name? Then why did you register as Stanley Langston? What is your relationship with the deceased? Then why were you traveling as Mr. and Mrs.? Those four questions alone could get him into serious trouble.

I want to help you, son. Please get in touch with me. Please.

My thoughts swung back and forth between the hysterical and the practical. I saw Steve slumped in the front seat of a car on a deserted country road, his body riddled with bullets. I saw him in a windowless room in a police station, surrounded by officers who were hurling questions at him. I saw myself hiring a lawyer to defend him. I saw myself explaining the whole thing in a straightforward manner to Edmund Burr, with Steve at my side filling in the details of Pepper's theft ring. I saw Pepper being arrested and led away in handcuffs. I saw Steve returning to the sort of life a young man of nineteen should be leading, either at school or in some line of work that offered a bright future.

I even saw Steve confessing to me that he was the one who'd killed Georgette.

That scene I turned away from completely. It wasn't true. It couldn't possibly be true.

The afternoon was a bad one. And at four-thirty it got even worse.

When the telephone rang I raced into the bedroom and

grabbed it in such a hurry that I dropped it. The call had to be from Steve. Simply because I wanted it to be.

It wasn't, though. It was from Rita. She too sounded on the verge of hysteria.

"I can't see you tonight, Walter. I'm going away. I'm packing right now. I—I'm going to St. Louis."

"St. Louis? What's the matter?"

"Nils phoned a little while ago. I—Ann's had an accident. She fell off a ladder. She has a broken leg, and I—they're afraid she's going to lose the baby." Her voice broke. "I'm—will you drive me to the airport, Walter? I'll be ready in five minutes."

I didn't know whether to say yes or no. I said no.

Rita said good-bye and hung up before I had a chance to tell her about Georgette. Her good-bye had been an angry one.

I started to call her back and explain. Then I decided that she had enough on her mind.

17

The five-o'clock news was a repeat of the three-o'clock news, with one addition. The police were attempting to locate Mrs. Langston's husband, who was in Chicago with her, but they hadn't yet succeeded in doing so.

I turned off the radio and turned on the television set. The story was also on television. There was a view of the body being carried from the motel to an ambulance, covered with a blanket. There was a view of the room, with a close-up of the blood-stained chair and carpet. There was a brief interview with the manager of the motel, who was explaining that Mr. and Mrs. Langston had checked in a week ago last Wednesday and that he didn't know anything about them.

There'd also been a big fire on the South Side. A mother and three children had burned to death.

I poured myself some more Scotch and went to the window. Darkness had fallen. All I could see were the lights of the cars on the Inner and Outer Drives and the reflection of my own face. The days are getting short, I thought. I could hear the voice of the commentator coming from the television set, but what he was saying didn't sink in.

I watched the lights of the cars. It seemed to me that the rush-hour traffic was worse tonight than usual. Then I remembered that it was Friday. The traffic was always bad on Fridays.

I closed my eyes and again saw the bloodstains on the chair and carpet, the ambulance attendants with their unrecognizable burden. I opened my eyes and turned away from the window.

The head of the teachers' union was being interviewed. The teachers were threatening to strike again. They wanted smaller classes.

I turned off the set. I took my glass into the kitchen and washed it.

Had Steve heard the news on the radio in his car? If so, what had his reaction been? To run?

I hoped not. He needed someone with him. Someone he could hang on to, no matter what happened. If he was still alive.

He had to be alive. He just had to be.

I leaned against the kitchen table. I thought that I ought to eat something. I hadn't eaten since breakfast. I wasn't hungry, though.

What had Ann been doing on a ladder? Didn't she know better?

Perhaps the news of the murder would be in the St. Louis papers, too. I'd have to call Rita in the morning.

My thoughts continued to ramble. The hope of hearing from Steve waned. What I had to do—really had to do—was get in touch with Burr. I wondered what time he'd be back from Springfield.

I walked into the living room and sat down at the desk. Fenwick's prescription was where I'd left it, along with the receipt from the hospital. I ought to get the prescription filled. I needed it.

I was still sitting at the desk when the doorbell rang. Who now? I thought. I sighed and got up to push the button, half expecting that the police had somehow found out I was the man in the plaid overcoat.

It wasn't a policeman who stepped out of the elevator, however. It was Steve. He was grinning.

"Guess what," he said before he even got to the door. "I found a job. Isn't that great?"

I put my arm around him. "Come inside," I said. "I have something to tell you."

18

At three o'clock I awoke. Sounds were coming from the bedroom. I got up from the couch and went to investigate.

Steve was murmuring in his sleep and moaning. I stood in the doorway for a moment, looking at him. He was curled up like a fetus, hugging the pillow. A corner of the pillowcase had worked its way between his lips. He appeared to be biting on it.

The bad dream he'd experienced consciously he was experiencing again in unconsciousness. Or perhaps this dream was even worse.

I was tempted to wake him, but before I could he turned restlessly onto his back and threw his left arm wide, and the murmuring stopped. I remained in the bedroom for another few moments, hoping that the few hours of troubled sleep would give him enough strength to face the day ahead, then went back to the living room and turned off the light.

If I'd raised him, I thought, I'd understand him. But I hadn't raised him and I didn't understand him. His reaction to the news of Georgette's death hadn't been what I'd expected. There'd been hardly any outward display of grief. He'd uttered one strangled sob, then withdrawn to some sanctuary deep within himself. His face had gone pale, his eyes had turned dark —he'd aged years in a matter of seconds. But he hadn't expressed his feelings vocally. I could only guess at his emotions. Just as I could only guess at the experiences that had taught him, at such an early age, not to admit to pain.

His surface calm made it easy to talk to him, however. I was able to explain how I'd followed him the night before and how I'd returned to the motel shortly before noon, hoping to find Georgette alone. He didn't become angry. He seemed to understand my wish to separate him from her.

We were able to talk about Pepper. I described the man who'd come to my apartment posing as a detective. That was Pepper, Steve assured me.

We speculated on how Pepper had found Georgette. It was pure speculation, but Steve was of the opinion that if the FBI knew that he and Georgette were in Chicago, then the Los Angeles police department also knew, and if the Los Angeles police department knew, there was every likelihood that Pepper had been tipped off.

Steve and Georgette had arrived in Chicago by plane. With no cash. Georgette had a girlfriend who lived in one of the suburbs—Skokie. The girlfriend's name was Sally Wayne. They'd called her from the airport and said they'd like to come over. They'd gone to her house directly from the airport. She'd loaned them a hundred dollars and her car. They'd found the Riverview Inn by chance, on their way into the city from Sally's house. They'd only kept the car for a day and a half. Georgette had been anxious to return it as soon as possible, since Pepper also knew Sally and might be able to trace them through her. During that day and a half they'd raised cash by selling a bracelet and a pair of earrings Georgette was wearing and they'd bought the car.

"Why did you have to have a car right away?" I asked.

"If we were going to stay here we'd need it to look for jobs and an apartment and everything. If we didn't stay here it was a way to move on."

"Couldn't you just rent one?"

"They won't rent you one without credit cards any more, and that's what we didn't have."

"No cash and no credit cards?"

"Georgette had money in a bank in Los Angeles. It was a question of getting it."

"Could Pepper have found out where you were from Sally?" Steve pondered.

"Did you tell her where you were staying?"

He shook his head. Then he remembered something. "Yes, he could."

"How?"

"When I called for a taxi." Georgette hadn't gone with him when he returned Sally's car. He'd driven it to Sally's house and taken a taxi back to the motel. Sally had given him the telephone number of one of the suburban taxi companies. In taking the order the dispatcher had asked him where he was going. There was something about suburban cabs driving within city limits. He'd given the dispatcher the name of the motel. Sally might have overheard. "I didn't even think of it until now," he said, and his eyes became even darker.

"What kind of woman is Sally Wayne?" I asked.

He didn't answer immediately. He was reliving something—perhaps his ride back to the motel in the taxi. "She seemed all right. She worked with Georgette for a while. She's divorced now." He thought about it some more. "She just didn't know, I guess."

"Once Pepper found out where you were staying, the rest would be easy."

He nodded.

"He must have found out only yesterday, though. He didn't know on Thursday, when he came to see me."

"It doesn't matter now."

As far as Georgette was concerned that was true. "I think he wants you out of the way too."

Steve looked at me. His expression was opaque. "Probably."

"Well, I'd just as soon he didn't find you."

"I'd kind of like to run into him."

"You're no match for him, Steve."

He said nothing.

"The one we're going to have to talk to is my friend at the FBI."

He didn't say anything to that either.

"You have to tell them everything you know."

Steve's silence continued.

"That's the only way."

"Call him," Steve said at last.

I called the FBI office. I left my name and the information that it was important for Mr. Burr to get in touch with me at once; the matter was urgent.

Burr didn't call me until almost ten o'clock. I told him that I had some information for him. I didn't tell him what the information was, but he seemed to know—it didn't take him long to agree to meet me. Would I come to the FBI office at ten in the morning? This wasn't his Saturday to work, but he would anyway. I said I'd be there. I also said that we'd better postpone the dinner on Monday night—Rita had gone out of town.

After talking to Burr I was relieved. I spent the rest of the evening trying to come up with words that would make Steve feel better. Whether any of them registered with him or not, I couldn't detect. He just sat there patiently, agreeing with me or saying nothing. Finally I stopped. At best all I was doing was conveying good intentions. And perhaps I was being a bore.

At midnight I offered him the use of my bed, and he accepted. I folded myself up on the couch.

From three to four I dozed fitfully. Steve moaned in his sleep several times. Once loud enough to bring me into the bedroom again. He didn't wake, however, and sometime after four I fell into a deep sleep myself. I didn't come out of it until seven.

Steve too was up by then. He was sitting on the bed, smoking a cigarette.

"Everything OK?" I asked.

He gave me a thin smile. He looked worse now than he'd looked during the evening. His eyes were red, and his face was dark with beard stubble. He seemed even thinner than he had before. A very old, very weary young man.

I went over to him and put my hand on his shoulder. He didn't say anything. I couldn't think of anything to say either. Nothing except, "There's shaving gear in the bathroom."

He nodded, put out his cigarette and went to shave. I got some coffee started.

Over toast and coffee he asked whether he was supposed to go to the FBI office with me.

My original plan had been to take him along, but during the wakeful moments of the night I'd reconsidered. The police were undoubtedly scouring the city for him. What was the relationship between the police and the FBI? The police had probably discovered by now, through a careful examination of the items in the motel room, that Georgette wasn't Mrs. Stanley Langston. And if she wasn't Mrs. Stanley Langston, they'd reason, then the man who was registered with her might not be Mr. Stanley Langston. That alone made things look bad. Although, from what Steve had told me, his job-hunting had given him a provable alibi for the time of the murder, the police could hold him for questioning. What that might lead to was anybody's guess.

It would be better if Burr would act as intermediary between Steve and the police. Better if Steve weren't booked. Better if he weren't locked in a cell, even for a fraction of a day.

"No," I said. "Let me lay the groundwork. If things work out the way I hope they will, you can go down there with me this afternoon and give them a complete statement."

He didn't seem to care one way or the other.

"Just don't get any ideas about leaving the apartment," I said.

100

"Not for any reason whatsoever."

He said nothing to that.

"Do I make myself clear?" I asked.

He nodded.

"Nothing you can do will bring Georgette back," I said.

He gazed out of the kitchen window.

I let some time elapse, then said, "Steve, in time your feelings will change. You'll get over her. What you have to do now is clear yourself of this mess and go on toward making a sensible life for yourself."

He turned his gaze back to me. There was more wisdom in his eyes that I'd believed he possessed. "I was already getting over her, Dad. But she didn't deserve to die. Not like that."

I let the matter rest. I went to bring in the newspaper.

One look at it was enough to convince me that my decision to see Burr alone was the right one. The story of the murder was on page one. MURDER VICTIM LINKED TO JEWEL RING was the headline. And under that, in type that was only slightly smaller, were the words: *Police Seek Missing Companion.*

I started to hide the newspaper before Steve could see it, but he came into the living room while I still had it in my hand.

"What does it say?" he asked.

There was nothing for me to do but show it to him.

He studied the story for a moment, then said sadly, "I'll never in a million years be able to prove I wasn't one of them."

"Yes you will," I said. But at that moment I wasn't at all certain.

19

Burr's manner was more impersonal than it had been before, and I felt less comfortable than I'd expected.

"Have you seen the morning paper?" I began.

He nodded. He kept his eyes on me.

"You told me to let you know if I heard from my son."

The same. A nod. No shift in the direction of his gaze.

"Well, I heard from him."

"When?"

"The day after you were in my office."

Burr didn't indicate how he felt about my not having told him before. "Go on," he said.

"I know I should have got in touch with you right away. I'm sorry now that I didn't. But at any rate I didn't, and now it's such a complicated story that I don't know where to begin."

He didn't tell me where to begin. He simply blinked and waited.

"Before I get started, though, there are a couple of points you might be able to clear up for me."

No help here either. Just attentive silence.

"First I'd like to know whether there's anything in the files that says Steve was a member of the gang that Georgette was spotting for."

Burr placed one hand on top of the other and stated his position. "I'm not officially on this case, Walter. I could get myself assigned to it if I wanted to but at the moment I'm not. I did volunteer to interview you, because I wanted to meet you, and I'm here this morning because we have a friendly relationship and I felt it would be easier for you to talk to me than to someone else. But it's not my case."

"Nevertheless, Ed."

"Nevertheless I can tell you this. I glanced through the file before you came in. There's nothing that says he is. I told you that before."

"OK. Next, if Steve came in and made a voluntary statement to you or to whoever is handling the case, would you turn him over to the Chicago police?"

"That would depend on what he said."

"He didn't kill her, Ed. That can be proved."

"Then what are you worried about?"

"I'm worried about Steve. About the effect all of this is going to have on him. I'm also worried because his life is in danger."

Burr's eyes narrowed perceptively. "Because he knows who killed her?"

"Yes. And because he knows more than that."

He leaned forward. "Why don't you just tell me the story, Walter, and let me decide how to handle it?"

"I want to tell you the story, Ed. I also want to protect Steve."

"A murder investigation is under way. I'm certainly not going to take it upon myself to obstruct that."

"I'm not asking you to. But can't I just bring Steve up here and let you take his statement, and you can give the police a copy of it? Steve wouldn't hold anything back."

"I'm afraid it's a bit more complicated than that. The FBI is investigating a ring of jewel thieves that has been based in

California. The Chicago police are investigating a murder that took place here. Even if the two are interrelated, there are jurisdictional problems."

I bit my lip and tried to figure out how to proceed. Things weren't going as I'd hoped. "I see."

Burr's expression softened slightly. "Walter, I'm not going to do anything to hurt you or your son. Neither is anyone else up here."

"I believe that. But the kid is in serious danger."

"If he's innocent, as you say, neither of you has anything to worry about."

I wasn't going to talk him out of a thing. I could see that. "I'm not so sure. There's a leak in the police department. Not here but in California. That's how Georgette got herself killed."

"Now we're getting someplace," Burr said. "But start at the beginning."

I did. I was already in too deep not to, and, having gone so far, there was nothing to be gained by leaving any of the facts out. I began with the bad checks, described Steve's involvement with Georgette, her dealings with her husband, Dave's confession and the leak in the police department, Pepper's attempt to kill Georgette in California, her flight with Steve to Chicago—I related everything, including the information that the overcoat I was wearing was the one in which I'd been seen at the motel.

Burr listened with deep concentration, interrupting only once or twice when I got ahead of myself.

I concluded with the point I'd made in the first place. "So you see why I say Steve's in danger."

"Where is he now?" Burr asked.

I'd told him everything else; I might as well tell him that too. "At my apartment."

"You'd better bring him down here."

I nodded. "What steps will you take to protect him?"

"Leave that to us."

"Will he have to go to the police?"

104

"They'll want to question him. And they'll want to verify his movements yesterday."

"If Pepper is caught, will Steve have to testify?"

"I should think so. Definitely. He'll be one of the key witnesses."

I sighed unhappily.

"Don't worry. We'll look after him. Now hold on a minute." Burr got up from his desk and left the office. He returned in a couple of minutes with two men. He introduced them as Carstairs and Doyle. They were the ones who'd done most of the work on the case, he said. He gave them a capsule version of what I'd told him. They asked a few questions of him and of me.

I asked a few questions myself. What I was mainly curious about was how the FBI had known that Steve and Georgette were in Chicago.

Carstairs explained that Georgette had been under surveillance for some time. The police had discovered a pattern in the robberies. While not all of the victims had patronized the beauty shop at which Georgette worked, most of them had. At first Georgette had been only one of the employees under suspicion. Then it was learned that she had a record. She'd been arrested twice—both times for attempting to sell stolen merchandise. In each case the charges had been dropped when the merchandise couldn't be positively identified. But on the basis of her history the police had begun to watch her. The problem was that they couldn't get any evidence against her.

"How did the FBI get in on the case?" I asked.

"The victims weren't all from California."

"You mean the gang operated outside of Los Angeles too?"

"We don't know exactly how many states they operated in, or how many people are involved outside of Los Angeles. So far we believe we've linked them to almost thirty crimes, with a total haul of over three million dollars."

I swallowed. "You must have known, then, that Georgette and Steve were at the motel in San Bernardino."

Carstairs shook his head. "Unfortunately, we didn't. They got out through a side entrance of the building they lived in. We didn't know where they were for over a week. Then we found out that they were here."

"How?"

"Through the car. The police had been looking for it. It was found in the parking lot at the airport. We began checking around the airport, and we found that they'd bought tickets for a flight to Chicago. Your son paid for them by check. He had plenty of identification. What he didn't have was enough money in the bank to cover the check."

"You mean he passed another bad check?"

Carstairs nodded.

"You didn't tell me that," I said to Burr. "Neither did Steve. I'll make the check good."

"It wasn't important," Burr said. "Livingston has already made the check good." He turned to Carstairs. "Isn't that right?"

"Yes," Carstairs said.

"Your son probably didn't even know that the check wouldn't clear," Doyle added. "I don't remember the exact amount, but there was something like fifty dollars less in his account than the amount of the check. The thing is, the airline had a record of the transaction, which made our job easy. They'd bought tickets to Chicago, so presumably they were here. But we didn't know where to start looking. We questioned Mrs. Livingston, and she suggested that the boy might try to get in touch with you. It often works that way, you know."

"He didn't want any money from me," I said. "I offered him some."

"It often works that way too," said Doyle. "I wouldn't be surprised if it was as much his doing that they picked Chicago as it was hers."

"She has a friend here," I said.

"She probably has friends elsewhere too," Doyle said. "In any event, he did look you up."

"True," I said.

106

"The thing we have to do now," Burr said, "is get him down here."

"I'll get in touch with L.A.," Carstairs said. "We want all the information we can get on this Pepper Himes."

"He'll get wind of it," I said.

"So he'll get wind of it," said Carstairs. "What time will you be back here with your son?"

"In an hour," I said.

They said they'd wait. All three of them.

I left. I wasn't altogether happy with the way things had gone but I felt better than I had at the beginning. I'd done what I had to. Now it was Steve's turn. And the FBI could offer him better protection than I could. He certainly wasn't safe in my apartment.

But when I got home, instead of finding Steve I found two members of the Chicago police department and a man with a cut lip. The man with the cut lip was Delmore Livingston.

20

The first policeman insisted on identifying himself. His name was Krakorski. "Are you the owner of this apartment?" he demanded.

"I live here," I said. I turned to Livingston. I'd only seen him once in my life. For maybe half a minute, more than a dozen years before, when he'd come into the room to back up Olive's statement that it would be impossible for me to see Steve. He hadn't changed much, though. He still reminded me of something that belonged in an aquarium. He was long and slim and silvery, like some species of eels. "What's going on?"

"My son struck me," he said as distinctly as the cut lip would permit.

"Where is he?" I snapped.

"He fled. I intend to press charges."

I looked at him. Then I looked at the two policemen.

"It's assault and battery," Krakorski said.

I directed my gaze at Livingston again. "Get rid of them," I said in a tight voice.

He started to object, but before he could get anything out I repeated my instructions. "Get rid of them." I was as angry as I'd ever been in my life. It must have showed.

"Now wait a minute," Krakorski said aggressively.

"Get rid of them," I said, pausing after each word.

"I'd like your full name," Krakorski said.

The other officer took a notebook from his pocket.

"Put that away," I told him. "This is my apartment. I did not call the police. There has been no violation of the law that I'm aware of." I turned back to Livingston. "I hope you have a good lawyer. You're going to need him."

Livingston dabbed at his lip with his handkerchief. There was a flicker of uncertainty in his eyes. I noticed it. So did Krakorski.

"There'll be no complaint signed," I told the policemen. "At most there was a slight family argument. I'm sorry that you were called away from your duty."

"This is our duty," Krakorski insisted.

"Tell them that it was just a slight family argument," I instructed Livingston. "That you won't sign a complaint."

Whatever else he was, the man was no fool. He recognized urgency when he encountered it. He also recognized a look that told him he'd made a terrible mistake. "Perhaps I was hasty," he said to Krakorski. "Let me think it over. Where can I get in touch with you?"

The policeman looked from one to the other of us. He appeared to be annoyed. He also appeared to realize that there was no point in wasting time if Livingston wasn't going to press charges. After a moment he gave Livingston a card and me a scowl. "Come on," he said to his partner. They left.

"How long ago did Steve take off?" I asked.

"About three quarters of an hour," Livingston replied. "That young scoundrel—"

"Get your coat. You're coming with me."

He drew himself up. "I'm going nowhere with you. That young—"

I wrapped my fingers around his arm and squeezed. I knew

I was hurting him. "I don't know how you got here," I said, "or what happened after you did get here, but I have a pretty good idea, and you're coming with me to the FBI office. Now."

It must have been difficult for him not to wince, but he didn't. He simply said, "Why there?"

I told him.

And he came with me.

21

Livingston refused to say a thing until he had a lawyer. It didn't take him long to get one, however. He placed a call to a country club in Palm Springs and asked for a Mr. Sabatini. When Mr. Sabatini came on the line Livingston said merely that he was at the FBI office in Chicago and needed a lawyer immediately. Within fifteen minutes Sabatini called back, and within another half-hour a lawyer appeared. The lawyer's name was Oscar Owen Nelson, and I'd read a lot about him. He'd represented a number of clients whose legal affairs were matters of national interest. He was an impressive-looking man with beetle eyebrows and he would have been even more impressive if he hadn't arrived at the FBI office with a dab of mustard at the corner of his mouth.

What Livingston wanted him for I couldn't figure out. Perhaps he was just accustomed to having lawyers around. In any event, he told as much with Nelson there as he would have told without him. His story was simple enough, and he told it in a straightforward manner.

He'd been notified that his son had passed another bad check and that the check had been written to pay for two plane tickets to Chicago. He'd been furious. He'd discussed the matter with his wife. She'd agreed with him that such irresponsible behavior couldn't be allowed to continue. Something would have to be done. He was the one to do it.

He made no attempt to justify himself. It was merely a matter of insufficient funds, he admitted, and the amount involved was less than fifty dollars. He'd undoubtedly overreacted. But on the other hand he'd had previous experiences with his son in which the amounts involved were larger and the intention was less innocent. The boy had to be made to realize that he was accountable for his actions and that financial dishonesty was intolerable. "I'm proud of my name," he said, "and I want my son to be proud of it too. But apparently in this particular case I erred."

Looking at it from his viewpoint, I had to admit that he hadn't done anything so very wrong. He'd already been questioned by the FBI about Steve's association with a woman suspected of having criminal associations. It was understandable that he'd feel that Steve was following a course which would eventually lead him into serious trouble. The mistake he'd made was in getting on a plane to Chicago with the intention of finding Steve and threatening him.

It struck me as strange at first that he considered the money aspect to be more serious than Steve's relationship with Georgette. But then I realized that that was just part of his makeup: nothing in the world was more serious than money. I also wondered why he'd let a week elapse between the time he'd learned about the check and the time he'd come to Chicago. There was an explanation for that too, though. He'd been sick with the flu. What puzzled me most, however, was how a man with his knowledge of the world would expect to find Steve in a city as large as Chicago when he didn't even know whether Steve was still there. So I asked him.

"This was where he'd bought tickets to," Livingston replied, "so this was the place to start. My first thought was to get in touch with you. If you didn't know anything or wouldn't tell me, then I intended to hire private investigators. Needless to say, my first thought turned out to be the right one."

"But what made you think he'd try to get in touch with me?"

The look that Livingston gave me was unfathomable. "I just did, that's all."

He'd arrived in Chicago the night before. He'd decided to come to my apartment rather than telephone. Steve had let him in, thinking that it was I who was at the door. The quarrel had started almost immediately. Livingston assumed responsibility for it. No sooner had he walked into the apartment, he said, than he began berating Steve. For past actions as well as present ones. Exaggerating the seriousness of his latest offense. Insisting that he was going to notify the authorities, as he put it. With the result that Steve hit him and ran out.

Unable to contain myself, I said, "Hadn't you seen the newspapers? Hadn't you seen the story on television?"

"I rarely watch television," Livingston said in a tone that indicated he considered the medium a blight. Then he came down off his high horse and said simply, "No, I didn't."

My opinion of him fluctuated as I listened. He might be arrogant, snobbish, insensitive—but he wasn't a liar and he had a conception of right and wrong. Too narrow a conception of them, perhaps, but nevertheless a conception. I couldn't blame him for being proud of his name—it was identified with some pretty worthwhile projects. On the other hand, his attitude toward Steve seemed to me to be harsh and punitive, and I suspected that it had always been so. Possibly he couldn't help it, but that didn't make it any less harmful.

I didn't like him. But I couldn't hate him. Despite the havoc he'd caused.

"The question now is," he concluded, addressing himself to Nelson, "how do we proceed?"

Nelson cleared his throat and appeared to be about to say something lawyerlike, but before he could get it out Livingston answered his own question. "I think I'd best contact a few friends," he said, and rattled off a list of names. The list included a senator, a cabinet member, two presidential advisors and a high official in the Department of Justice. It was probably an oversight that he omitted the heads of the Joint Chiefs of Staff, the CIA and the Pinkerton and Hargrave detective agencies.

The three FBI agents may have been impressed but to their credit they didn't show it. "I'm afraid that in the end it will still come down to us, Mr. Livingston," Carstairs said. "We're the ones who'll have to find your son."

"I'd like to help," he said.

"We'll keep you advised," Doyle said.

Burr glanced at me and said, "Don't worry."

"I wish there were something I could do," I said.

"If there is," Burr promised, "I'll let you know."

My part in the meeting seemed to have come to an end. I got up to leave. They asked Livingston to stay, to answer some additional questions.

A final thought occurred to me. "Those two policemen who were at my apartment, Krakorski and the other one—"

"Don't worry about them," Burr said. "We'll take care of it."

I had to pass Livingston to get to the door. As I did our eyes met, and for an instant I got strange vibrations from him. It seemed almost as if he was jealous of me.

I said nothing. I reached the door and kept going.

Back to an apartment that seemed suddenly very empty.

22

In an attempt to establish some link with normalcy I placed a call to Rita in St. Louis.

She was at the hospital. I spoke with Nils, who'd just come from there. Ann hadn't lost the baby, but her leg was badly fractured; it would be in a cast for at least six weeks. What had she been doing on a ladder? I asked. Changing a light bulb, he replied. It was nice to hear the voice of a cheerful, uncomplicated young man who worked for a bank and liked what he was doing, was crazy about his wife and never got angry except when the Cardinals lost a game.

He made no mention of Steve or of the fact that I'd been sick, so I guessed that Rita hadn't had much to say about me. I asked him how soon she'd be back at the house, and he said in about an hour—he was taking her out to dinner. I told him to tell her to call me, and he said he would.

She didn't.

I called her a second time. There was no answer.

I tried to shut Steve out of my mind. I couldn't. It was a week to the day since he'd reappeared in my life, and in that week I'd become so involved with him that I'd lost my perspective. But then, my perspective had been shot to hell before he arrived.

Look at it this way, I told myself. The FBI has a staff of thousands. Delmore Livingston has assets of maybe a quarter of a billion. That's a powerful combination. Furthermore, Livingston's connections will affect the handling of the case; more men will be assigned to it than would be otherwise. Steve is only a nineteen-year-old kid, barely out of high school, with nothing but the clothes on his back and the few dollars in his pocket. He can't run far. They're bound to find him within a day.

My thoughts rambled along in that vein for a while, and I felt better. But when I thought of the figure I'd seen in the motel room with her face shattered I stopped feeling good.

I seesawed back and forth between self-induced optimism and the wildest kind of morbidness. I couldn't achieve any sort of balance.

The hardest part of it all was the inactivity. I wanted to go out and do something—anything—to help. To conduct my own house-to-house search. To drive up one street and down another. To cover some angle that the FBI might overlook. I couldn't come up with anything practical, however, and I knew that it wasn't smart to leave the apartment. There was still the chance that Steve might try to contact me.

At ten o'clock I called St. Louis for the third time. Rita was back from dinner. At first her voice was cold. Then I told her why I hadn't been able to drive her to the airport, and it warmed up.

"The poor thing," she said of Georgette.

"They'll find him," she said of Steve.

She was sympathetic enough. But I sensed that the situation wasn't quite real to her. Separated from it by almost three hundred miles, preoccupied with her own problems, she couldn't fully understand the turmoil. Which was a good thing.

Some of her detachment communicated itself to me and calmed me down.

"How long are you going to be there?" I asked.

"I don't know," she replied. "I don't want to leave just yet."

She gave me the most sensible advice I'd had all day. Get a good night's sleep, she said. Things will sort themselves out by morning.

They didn't. But I felt less disturbed.

I stood for a moment at the window, a mug of coffee in my hand. The sky was gray and seemed to merge with the lake just beyond the beach. There was a lack of traffic and a stillness in the air that occurred only on Sunday mornings. The snow, no longer clean, had started to melt.

I put the mug down and brought in the newspaper. The story of the murder had been relegated to page nine and it wasn't much of a story. QUESTION GUESTS IN MOTEL SLAYING was the headline. The guests referred to were the other occupants of the motel. The only new information that the police had to offer was that a salesman from Minneapolis whose name was Richard Allen claimed he'd heard something that sounded like gunshots at around ten-thirty on the morning of the murder.

There was no mention of Steve or of the man in the plaid overcoat, and I guessed that someone from the FBI had passed the word along to the Police Department to play down those points. The article did give Georgette's correct name and did say that she was the estranged wife of a former Los Angeles policeman. They had his name right too. Francis Himes.

I read what the sports writers had to say about the day's games and tried to pick the winners. I picked the Rams, the Vikings and the Cowboys. As it sometimes did on Sunday mornings, my mind took a brief trip backward in time. I was living in a big house in Benedict Canyon, and my wife was pregnant. It was a hot morning, and we were having breakfast in the patio. She had a ribbon around her hair. The ribbon was blue.

Suddenly I came back to the present. I put the newspaper aside and went to the telephone. I placed a call to Mrs. Delmore Livingston in Bel-Air, California.

I didn't reach her. A high-pitched male voice told the operator, "Missy Lilingston not here. Missy Lilingston go out of town." The operator told me, and I canceled the call. I wondered where Olive had managed to find a Missy-Lilingston type of houseman. Even twenty years ago they'd been rare.

I tried the Ambassador, the Astor Towers and the Drake. At the Drake I connected. Livingston was registered there, but his line was busy. I waited. After a while I got through.

"Walter Jackson," I said. "I just wanted to know if you've heard anything."

"I've been on the phone to Washington," Livingston replied, which didn't answer my question. He didn't sound unfriendly. Merely stiff. "I've had no direct news of Steve, if that's what you mean," he added. "Have you?"

"No, I haven't."

There was a silence. I couldn't think of anything to say but I couldn't bring myself to hang up. Apparently he was having the same problem. "If you'd care to come over," he said presently.

I didn't want to leave the apartment, in case Steve tried to reach me. On the other hand, I didn't know how much longer I'd be able to stay in the apartment alone without losing my sanity, and the prospect of Steve's trying to reach me was getting dimmer by the minute. Maybe Livingston would think of something he hadn't thought of before. Or I would. I said, "For a little while, perhaps."

"Good."

I shaved and showered. While showering I got another idea. Steve might have tried to contact Sally Wayne. I'd told the FBI men about her; they'd probably paid her a visit. But possibly she'd tell me something she hadn't told them.

The idea didn't come to anything. There was no telephone listing for a Mrs. Sally Wayne in Skokie. Was it possible, the information operator suggested, that she was listed under a different spelling? I wasn't sure of the spelling, and it was more than likely that the telephone was still listed in the name of her ex-husband, and I didn't know the address or even the name of the street. There was nothing to do but give up.

I dressed and drove to the Drake.

Livingston was in the kind of suite you'd expect him to be in. It overlooked the lake, and you went down a couple of steps to enter the living room. His lip was swollen, and there were shadows under his eyes. I guessed that he wasn't having any better time than I was.

He'd ordered up coffee, he said, and led me to a table by the window. I didn't want any coffee but I drank some anyway. His manner was the same as it had been on the telephone—stiff but not unfriendly. He mentioned the names of some of the important people he'd spoken to. Most of them couldn't possibly be of any help, it seemed to me. But at least he was trying. And I gathered that he simply didn't know of any other way in which to operate. To accomplish anything, you had to deal with someone at the top—even if the person might be at the top of the wrong outfit.

"As far as you know," I said, "does Steve have any friends here in Chicago? Can you think of anyone he might go to for money or just for a place to stay?"

Livingston shook his head slowly. "That's what they kept asking me yesterday. They kept me in that office until almost five o'clock, questioning me about Steve's friends and activities. I wasn't very helpful, I'm afraid. I just don't know."

He'd raised him. He'd lived under the same roof with him for fifteen years. He'd made him his son. But he didn't know. "That's the trouble with living in a big house," I said. "People never meet."

"I haven't failed at most things," Livingston said. "Just at that one." He looked at me. It was the same sort of look he'd given me as I was leaving the FBI office and it had the same effect on me. Made me think that I had something he wanted.

"I missed him very much over the years." I said.

Livingston gazed at his costly view of the lake for a moment, then at his coffee cup. "He missed you too, I think."

"I never got that impression," I said.

He flushed and put the cup down. "I felt that you were a bad influence."

"Apparently." He doesn't really remind me of an eel, I thought. There's nothing slippery about him.

He glanced over my shoulder. "Good morning," he said.

I turned. And spilled a quarter of a cup of coffee.

Olive came down the steps. "Walter," she said with a smile.

I hastily put my cup on the table and wiped the coffee from my hand with a handkerchief. A lot of emotions hit me, all at the same time.

She brushed her present husband's cheek with her lips and shook her ex-husband's damp hand.

She'd had long brown hair, the softest hair I'd ever touched. And large brown eyes which made her appear to be ever vulnerable. And a round face, with full lips. The long brown hair was now grayish white and short, like a boy's. The eyes were still large, but the effect wasn't so much one of vulnerability as one of anxiety. The face had become more angular. She was only forty-one but she looked fifty-five.

I tried to smile. I couldn't.

"It's been a long time," she said.

I nodded. Every fond recollection I'd had of our years together now seemed distorted. Had she ever been as I'd remembered? "When did you get to town?" I finally managed to ask.

"Last night. Or, rather, this morning. After Delmore called, I took the last flight. Flying at night always did frighten me and it still does."

The love, the hurt, the rage—they recurred simultaneously, and vanished simultaneously. In their place came confusion.

"You've changed very little, Walter."

It was probably a lie. As much of a lie as a remark like that

120

about her would have been, coming from me. "I don't know," I said.

I cast a furtive glance at Livingston. Was it possible that this thin, silver-haired, arid, troubled multimillionaire destroyed everyone who came close to him? It appeared that way.

"We were talking about Steve," he told Olive.

A shadow crossed her face. "I'm afraid we've made mistakes with Steve."

"I've acknowledged that," Livingston observed dryly.

"I was asking whether there's anyone here he might have got in touch with," I said.

"Delmore and I went over that last night," Olive said. "I simply don't know of anyone."

"Didn't you have any contact with him at all during the past year?"

"It's different today from when we were young," she said, making it sound as if a hundred years had passed since we were young. And it wasn't so different at that, I thought: she'd eloped with me against her father's wishes. "If one's children take it upon themselves to leave home and lead their own lives, they do." She turned to Livingston. "At least ours did."

I felt a flash of resentment. She was as much as saying that Steve was his and hers, not hers and mine. "I think you might have made an effort to locate him," I said sharply.

She was taken aback. She recovered. "Oh, we knew where he was. The De Lisos are neighbors of ours."

"The De Lisos are the parents of the young man Steve was staying with in Malibu," Livingston explained.

"And you didn't go out there to see him?" I asked Olive.

"Once," she replied. "The house was quite attractive." She paused. "Steve was on the beach with some other young people. Someone went to get him. He came into the house. He refused to speak to me except to tell me to go home. He was really quite rude."

"And after that?"

"I met him once, by accident. He was walking on Rodeo Drive with my manicurist."

"Your manicurist?"

"Mrs. Himes used to do Olive's nails," Livingston said.

I looked from one to the other of them.

"It was quite embarrassing," Olive said.

"Do the FBI know that?" I asked Livingston.

"I told them, back in California," he said.

"It was so awkward," Olive said. "I scarcely knew what to say. Naturally I changed manicurists."

I was at a loss for words.

"We simply had no control over him, you see," Olive added.

I thought of the hundreds of desperate hours we'd put in at Cedars of Lebanon Hospital, waiting to learn whether our child had survived the most recent operation and whether he'd ever be normal. That must have been a different Olive, I thought; no relation to this one. "You've changed a great deal," I said.

Again she was taken aback. "That doesn't quite sound like a compliment." Again she recovered, though. "You can hardly expect me to be proud of the fact that my son is keeping company with my manicurist."

"Olive is a bit narrow-minded," Livingston put in. "I think it's good for young men at a certain age to have experiences with different kinds of women. You don't want them to grow up to be snobs."

I felt that there was no way in the world for me to answer either one of them. "Would you happen to know the name of the owner of the shop?" I asked Olive.

"Before or after?" she said.

"Before or after what?" I asked.

"Before or after it changed hands. It changed hands two or three years ago. The new owner is Victor. The old one was Pablo. Why?"

"I just wondered."

"Victor isn't as good as Pablo was. A lot of people like him, though. As for myself, I always thought that Pablo was better.

So did Mother. He was less temperamental. Perhaps because he was only half Spanish. The other half was English."

"What happened to him?"

"I don't know. He left California, I believe. Moved somewhere else." Her expression changed. Something had registered with her. "To Chicago, as a matter of fact."

"Would you happen to remember his last name?"

She thought for a moment. It came to her. "Wayne."

"Was his wife's name Sally?"

Olive was surprised. "How did you know?"

"Someone mentioned the name. It may have been Georgette."

Olive was even more surprised. "You met Georgette?"

"Why, yes," I said. "She and Steve had dinner with me the other night. She was a lovely-looking woman, don't you think?"

Olive's expression was that of someone who'd just seen a roach. "That would depend upon one's taste," she replied.

23

"I need a favor," I said.

"Sure, Walter," Charly Kipness said. "Anything."

"You have a client in the beauticians'-supply business, don't you?"

"Right."

"I'm trying to locate a particular beauty operator, and he's not listed in the telephone directory, and all the beauty shops are closed today. Do you think your man could find out where he lives?"

"I could ask him."

"The man's name is Pablo Wayne. He owned a shop in Los Angeles or Beverly Hills. He sold it a couple of years ago and moved here. He was divorced recently, and before the divorce he lived in Skokie."

"Larry may have heard of him. Or if he hasn't, maybe he knows of someone else who might have. I'll see."

"Thanks. It's important. I need the information yesterday."

124

"Gotcha. By the way, Walter, what we were talking about the other day—"

"I meant it. But first things first. And the first thing at the moment is Pablo Wayne."

"Right." Charly rang off.

I crossed my fingers.

It was a long wait. At least thirty minutes. The slower variety of minutes. I was just getting ready to place a second call to Charly when the telephone rang.

Come through for me, baby, I thought as I lifted the instrument.

"Larry hadn't heard of him but he called a friend of his, and *he* had."

"Did he have the address?"

"I should hope so. He got him the apartment." Charly told me where it was. It was a neat four blocks from where I was standing.

"Thanks," I said. "I love you." And before he could get on to the subject of my turning my clients over to him I said, "We'll get together tomorrow or the next day and go over things." Then I hung up.

I called the FBI office to report my find.

Burr was out. Carstairs was out. Doyle was out.

I went out also. To the northern fringe of Old Town. To a three-story house which had once been very nice, had subsequently gone to pot and then been restored by someone who had artistic inclinations and liked glass bricks.

What had been the foyer of the house had been converted into the vestibule of an apartment building. There were three mailboxes on one wall, each with a slot for a nameplate, and below each mailbox was a button. I pushed the middle button. The nameplate above it said P. WAYNE.

A glass door separated the vestibule from a flight of stairs. The door wasn't locked. I opened it and began to climb. From somewhere above me a voice called, "Who is it?"

"Walter Jackson," I called back.

There was a silence. I kept climbing. And when I got to the second floor I found him standing in the doorway.

"Who are you, and what's your gig?" he said. "And unless you're the man with the mirror, I'm not interested. Are you the man with the mirror?"

"No," I said. "I'm the man with the problem. I'm not selling anything. All I want is to ask you a few questions. My ex-wife used to be a customer of yours."

"I didn't do it," he said.

"Mrs. Delmore Livingston," I said.

He came to attention, at least facially. "Olive Livingston?"

I nodded.

He didn't open the door any wider. But he didn't close it either. "How is she?" he asked.

"Not bad," I replied. "May I come in?"

He looked me over, then said, "I guess so," and stepped aside.

The apartment was in the process of being furnished. It had some items but not others. Everything was white. The paint on the walls, a rug made from the skin of a polar bear, a Bombay commode and one chair—all white. I could understand Pablo's interest in a man with a mirror.

"It'll be out of this world when it's finished," he said. "White is my astral color."

"It's nice now," I said.

"You from California?" he asked.

"Yes," I said.

"I was big out there. But I guess you know. And I'm going to be just as big here."

He came on breezier than he really was, I thought. More confident than he really was. His physique was small. He was no more than five feet seven inches tall and weighed maybe a hundred and thirty pounds. His shoulders were bony, his chest was hollow, and he had a triangular face which was made more triangular by a small black beard which came to a point. Yet in an odd way he was attractive. The beard, the alert black eyes, the curly hair—he made a favorable enough impression so that he didn't have to knock himself out with people the way he evidently did.

"So what do you see?" he asked.

I said the first thing that came into my mind. "A young Don Quixote."

He erupted into laughter. "I've been called a lot of things but never that."

"In the days before he began tilting at windmills," I added.

He laughed some more, then said, "Are you really Olive Livingston's ex-husband?"

"I am. She's the one who gave me your name."

"What do you want?"

"I'm trying to locate my son. Mrs. Livingston's son."

"Steve?"

"You know him?"

"I've met him." The traces of amusement vanished. His expression became guarded.

"He came to Chicago recently with a young woman who used to work at your shop. Georgette Himes."

"Georgette Himes drew the ten of hearts the other day. I read about it in the newspaper."

"I know. Steve wasn't with her at the time, but they had traveled here together."

Pablo shoved his hands into the pockets of his jeans. "I don't know what you're leading up to but I don't think I'm going to like it. As far as I'm concerned, Georgette was bad news. I owe her quite a bit, and none of it good."

"I'm really not leading up to anything specific, Pablo—I hope you don't mind my calling you that. But when they first got here Steve and Georgette did go to see your ex-wife, and what with one thing and another I thought you might be able to tell me something about Georgette that would help me locate Steve."

"Like what?"

"Anything. Did you ever meet her ex-husband—Pepper Himes?"

Pablo's skin was naturally dark. But it suddenly got darker. His eyes narrowed. "Look, Mr. Jackson, I let you in here, but that doesn't mean—"

"Please, Pablo. I came here because I really need help. Tell me whatever you can about Georgette."

Pablo eyed me for what seemed a long time, then shrugged and without a word went into the next room. He returned with a tall stool. He nodded to a chair and said, "Sit down." He himself perched on the stool.

"I had a good shop," he said. "The best in Beverly Hills. Ask anybody. I did movie stars and TV people, and they used to invite me to their parties, and my operators were the best. Mrs. Livingston probably told you."

I nodded.

"Well, it's on account of Georgette that I don't have it any more. I sold it for peanuts compared to what it was worth. All because of Georgette. A business like that you don't build just anywhere, any time." He paused, to give me time to challenge him if I wanted to.

I didn't.

"Well, when Monica quit I needed another girl and I hired Georgette. She seemed OK, and Sally knew her. Sally was my other manicurist. She'd been with me almost since I got started —I hired her away from Bruce O'Connor—and I ended up being married to her for a while. Anyway, she'd met Georgette and she said she thought she was OK, and I hired her. She was good too, Georgette was—don't get me wrong. My customers liked her—she had a way about her, I'll say that. After a while she got to be more popular than Sally, which Sally didn't exactly care for, but I was glad I had her—Georgette. The girls can give you almost as much trouble as the men can, but Georgette never did. You know anything about beauticians?"

"Not very much."

"Well, the customers don't give you nearly as much of a hard time as the operators do. I've done hair since I was sixteen years old and started working in my mother's place, and I know. But

128

Georgette was nice to everybody, and sometimes when I had trouble with one of the operators or they had trouble with each other she helped me straighten things out. She was good at that. Getting along with people, I mean. And she was smart." He put his elbows on his knees and leaned forward.

He really did put me in mind of a latter-day Spanish cavalier, I thought. Despite the jeans and the tank top and the hollow chest.

"Well, after a while things began to happen. You read in the paper that Georgette was mixed up with a ring of second-story men. Or maybe you knew it before. At any rate, my customers were getting robbed, and one of them—her husband was shot. These men were waiting for them in the garage of their house when they came home from a party one night, and the husband tried to be a hero, and one of the men shot him."

"The man die?"

"Not quite, but almost. At first I didn't think there was anything strange. I mean, the kind of women I had as customers, they were the kind who were always getting robbed or having things disappear on them. Some of them seemed kind of proud of it in a way. But after a while I began to wonder why it was happening more often. It *was* happening more often. The women would talk about it to each other—some of them even bragged about it. They liked the excitement, I think—having the police come around, and the insurance people and all that —but they were scared too. No one connected it with my shop, but they did feel that the area was getting dangerous, and they were having burglar alarms installed and hiring private watchman services and that sort of thing, and they were talking about that almost as much as they were talking about who was getting a divorce and who was giving a party."

"When did you begin to think that Georgette had something to do with it?"

"When the police began asking questions. They're pretty good at that sort of thing, some of them. The first thing they ask about is the household help, if there is any. But then they begin

129

asking about parties and friends and where the women shop and things like that. Most of the time they don't recover the stuff that was stolen, but they do find certain patterns, and they know that some places are more dangerous for women to hang around than others, or to wear their jewelry to. You'd be surprised."

"So eventually they came to you."

Pablo nodded. "Several times. They questioned me and they questioned my people."

"Including Georgette?"

"Including her. And I questioned my people too. Most of them I knew pretty well—I usually knew them before I hired them—but I began asking questions anyway."

"And you narrowed it down to Georgette?"

"Georgette and Deborah."

"Deborah?"

"She was the maid, or maybe I ought to say the cook. She helped the women dress and she served lunch. She made the food at home and brought it down with her every day." He paused and seemed lost in memories. A man whose present wasn't as good as his past. "She was a widow with three kids and she was having a tough time, so I thought it might be her. Especially when she quit." He paused again. "She didn't like the idea of my questioning her, so she quit and went to work for Bruce O'Connor. He'd been trying to get her for a couple of years. When she quit I thought it was because she was guilty. But then there was another robbery, and after a while the police came around again, so I knew I was wrong. I fired Georgette. And that was when the trouble started."

"Started?"

"For me, that is. Georgette's husband paid me a visit. He wanted to know why I'd fired her. I'd never met the guy, but there was something about him that I didn't like. He wasn't tacky or anything, but I didn't like the idea of his coming around like that to ask me why I'd fired her, and I kind of had the feeling that he wanted to make an issue over it. Then he asked me who'd replaced her. I didn't think it was any of his business and I didn't say much but I did say something, I guess, about having hired Tricia. He didn't say anything to that. All he said was that he thought I'd made a mistake. But when Tricia got attacked I couldn't help wondering whether he didn't have something to do with it."

"Tricia got attacked?"

It had happened late at night, Pablo explained. The girl had come home from a date. When she walked into her apartment she found two men there. They jumped her, and while one held her the other beat her. She ended up with a broken nose, two broken ribs, cuts and bruises all over her body and an internal hemorrhage that almost cost her her life.

A similar misfortune befell Kathleen, the girl who took Tricia's place. Not inside the apartment this time, but in an alley outside. And while Kathleen's injuries weren't as serious as Tricia's they were serious enough.

"You connected that with Georgette's husband too?"

"I didn't have to," Pablo replied. "He told me. Not in so many words, of course, but he came around again and said that since I seemed to be having such bad luck with my manicurists maybe I ought to hire Georgette back."

"You didn't report it to the police?"

"Report it to the police? He *was* the police, for God's sake! I didn't know he'd been kicked off the force. Georgette had always said that her husband was a policeman, and he said he was a policeman, and even if he wasn't a policeman what good would it have done me to go to the police? I couldn't prove anything. I'm damn sure that he wasn't the one who beat up those girls. I don't even think it was the same men who beat up both of them. According to what I heard, the men were different. But I was damn sure that Pepper Himes had something to do with both beatings."

"Did you hire Georgette back?"

Pablo put his head in his hands and stared at his polar-bear rug. "Yes." After a few moments he got up from the stool and walked across the room. Then he came back. "I also sold the business when Pepper came around again."

I stared at him. "Georgette's husband bought your beauty shop?"

"That's right. Him or someone he knew. Georgette was only there for a little while the second time when he showed up one night as I was closing and said that he had a friend who wanted to buy the place. Naturally I said I wasn't interested. I was clearing almost a hundred grand a year, I don't mind telling you. Again he said that he thought I was making a mistake. I might have an accident or something, and then where would I be? I was plenty scared, but I still said no."

"Was Georgette in the shop at the time?"

"No. She'd gone. I was alone. Then about a week later I was coming home—Sally and I were married then, and we had a house at Palos Verdes—well, just as I was about to go inside these two men came out of nowhere and began to rough me up. They didn't hurt me much, but I got the message. The next day Victor Tildon called and said that he'd like to buy my shop. I sold it to him. But I knew Victor from way back. He's a good operator but he never had two nickels to rub together. The place may be in his name, but it wasn't his money that bought it."

"I can't believe you didn't know Pepper wasn't a policeman any longer."

"I didn't, and that's the honest-to-God truth. I didn't know it until I read it in the newspaper here, yesterday."

"You'd met other policemen. They'd been around your shop."

"And they hadn't caught a single one of the robbers. And I was damn sure they couldn't help me. There's no real protection they could give me, not against somebody getting me alone somewhere and beating me senseless. It isn't even much of a crime, the way things are. Even if I'd known Georgette's husband wasn't a policeman I don't think I'd have done anything different. The way things turned out, I'm sure I did the right thing." He paused. "Look what happened to Georgette. Something like that might have happened to me if I'd tried to get smart. I'd rather sell my business than be dead." He worked his hands into the pockets of his jeans again and stood there, all hunched up. "It was a nice place, though. Vincent Lee Remington did it for me. He's a friend of mine. It was all white, except for one wall which was smoked glass." He sighed.

"It's a shame," I agreed. Business gone. House gone. Wife gone. I knew what it was like.

He came out of his reverie. "Did you find out what you came for?"

I really hadn't. "Can you give me any idea where Steve might have gone? Is there anyone he and Georgette might have known here, other than your wife or you?"

"If I'd known Georgette was in town, I think I'd have split. And I'm surprised that Sally saw her. She knew the story as well as I did. Unless she was afraid."

That was probably it, I thought. Not friendship, but fear.

"I'm sorry about your son, but I can't help you." He suddenly grinned. "You didn't see a man with a mirror on the way over here, did you?"

"Afraid not," I said with a smile. "There's one thing you can give me, though. Your ex-wife's address and telephone number."

He gave them to me. I wrote them down and hoisted myself out of the chair. "Thank you," I said.

"Don't thank me. You said I'm Don Quixote. That's enough. The Man of La Mancha. I'll remember that." He walked me to the door, humming.

We shook hands, and I left. As I walked back to my apartment the tune he'd hummed echoed in my ears. I tried to think of the name of it. At first it wouldn't come to me. Then it did. "The Impossible Dream."

24

The three FBI men were as unavailable at two-thirty as they'd been at a quarter to one. I had a strong hunch that they wouldn't be available at four or five or six, either, and that the soonest I'd be able to talk to any of them would be Monday morning.

Did Steve call while I was out? I asked the telephone.

The telephone had nothing to say. It sat there in glum silence.

He didn't, I decided. He won't. He might even think that I'm the one who told Livingston where to find him. He doesn't trust anyone at the moment.

I had two choices: I could wait or I could act.

The wait would be intolerable.

It was a nice house. Yellow brick. Split-level. Attached garage. Corner lot. Appraisable for insurance purposes at maybe forty thousand.

The drapes were drawn. The garage door was closed.

I rang the bell. I could hear the chimes ring on the inside. Do, re, mi, do.

Nothing happened.

I rang again.

At one side of the picture window the drape moved.

I turned down the collar of my overcoat and was about to touch the bell for the third time when the door opened. One full inch. On the safety chain.

"Who is it?" a woman's voice asked.

"Steve Livingston's father," I said.

An eye and a nose appeared in the opening.

"You're either going to have to talk to the FBI or to me," I said. "It might be better if you talked to me." I didn't know whether it would work or not, but there was a fifty-fifty chance.

It did. After a period of indecision she unhooked the safety chain and said, "Come in."

For some reason I'd made up my mind in advance what she'd look like: she'd look like Georgette. But she didn't. She was an attractive woman—a green-eyed blonde—but she reminded me more of Olive than of Georgette. The same short hair style, the same air of having had some of the vital juices dry up before they should have.

"I'm trying to find Steve," I said.

"They haven't found him yet?" she asked.

I wasn't sure who she meant by "they" but I guessed that she meant the police. "No," I said.

She led me into the living room. Pablo had evidently supervised the decorating. Everything was white. His astral color. Except for the cigarette butts in the ashtrays—all of them had vivid red lipstick stains on them. There were a lot of them, too. She took a fresh cigarette from a package in the pocket of her blouse and lit it. "I don't know where he is. I haven't seen him since right after they got here." She exhaled smoke and eyed me through it. "He looks like you."

"I know."

"What does the FBI want with me?"

"To question you about Georgette."

"How did they find out about me?"

"I told them."

She didn't ask how or when or why. She accepted it. "I suppose I ought to feel sorry that Georgette is dead. I don't, though. I've got some Bloody Mary mix. Would you like a Bloody Mary?"

"No, thanks."

"I think I'll have one." She added some ashes to the accumulation in one of the ashtrays and left the room.

I looked around. White drapes, white couch, antique white end tables. White carpet and white walls, except for one wall which was hung with smoked glass. The poor guy, I thought; he tried to bring his dream with him. I changed my mind about the Bloody Mary.

"I'll have that drink," I called.

"OK," Sally replied.

She returned presently with two glasses. "Did you know Georgette?" she asked as she handed me one.

"I met her."

"She seemed nice, didn't she?"

"You couldn't help liking her. But 'nice'—I don't know. That might be the wrong word."

"No. Everyone always thought she was nice. Including me for a while. At the shop she was everybody's favorite." She took a couple of long swallows of her drink. "Can you imagine someone like that getting tied up with a kid like Steve?"

"It happened."

"I know. I can't understand it. He's such a kid. He might have been her kid brother."

"I think she loved him."

"I only saw them together for a little while. But I think you're right. A kid like that. He might have been her kid brother."

"Maybe that's why she loved him."

"Maybe." She drank some more. "I don't like to think about

it. It gives me the creeps. It must give you the creeps too."

"I'd like to find him. Before something happens to him."

"The police think he did it?"

I shrugged. I drank some of the Bloody Mary. It wasn't bad. "He probably did. I wouldn't blame him."

"I don't think he did it. I think her husband did it."

Sally had been about to put the glass to her lips. Now she lowered it. "What do you know about him?"

"What Steve told me. And what your ex-husband told me."

She put the glass on a table. Carefully. "You've seen Pablo?"

"Yes."

"When?"

"This afternoon."

"I mean, why?"

"I thought he might be able to help me. Steve's mother gave me his name."

"I see. Well. In that case." She seemed suddenly to become aware of all of the cigarette butts in the ashtrays. She emptied two of the smaller ashtrays into one of the larger ones and left the room with it.

When she returned a few moments later the large ashtray was empty and she was smoking another cigarette. "Everyone thinks that just because you're divorced you don't like your ex. That's not true. I don't dislike Pablo. I feel sorry for him but I don't dislike him. What did he say about me?"

"He said that you recommended Georgette to him."

"Did he? Well, I suppose I did. I mean, I knew her. I'd known her off and on for a couple of years. At one time we lived in the same building."

"Was she married at the time?"

"She got married while she was living there."

"Then you must know Pepper."

Sally nodded.

"What's your opinion of him?"

She noticed her unfinished drink and picked it up. "What did Pablo tell you?"

"That Pepper gave him a hard time."

"Well, that's true. Pepper put him out of business. Nothing was the same after that. We came here and—well, it just wasn't the same. Yes, Pepper gave him a very hard time, and me too if you want to look at it that way. But I don't know. I think Georgette is to blame. I think that when she married him he was nice. I think she's the one who ruined him. She made him dishonest, I think. He eventually got fired from his job, and I think that after that he just went from bad to worse. When Georgette was going with him, before they got married, he wasn't like that. He was a nice, big, good-looking policeman who didn't seem to have any problems. But after he got fired from his job—well, I guess Pablo told you."

"A man doesn't get thrown off the police force for nothing."

"No. But it was Georgette's fault. She gave him ideas."

"Were you surprised when Georgette called you and said she was in town?"

Sally laughed. If you can call it laughing. Mostly it was an expression of bitterness and tension. "Surprised? That's one for the books. I was scared!" She finished her drink. "I didn't know she even knew where I was. I'd kept up with some of my friends in California but I hadn't kept up with her. One of them must have given her my phone number, but I don't know who. After what happened in California we thought it'd be a good idea to have an unlisted number. Pablo was still nervous. Anyway, out of the blue the phone rings and it's Georgette. She's just come in town with a friend of hers, and can she come over? I was afraid to say no. Actually afraid. Look at all the trouble she'd caused. You can't tell me that she didn't know what Pepper was up to. So I said yes. Then she and your son show up, and I think she's out of her mind—a kid like that. Nothing against him, you understand, Mr. Livingston, but nevertheless."

"Mr. Jackson," I said.

"Jackson?"

"Walter Jackson. Steve was adopted by Livingston, but I'm his real father."

138

"Oh. I didn't know that."

"Does it make a difference?"

"No, I suppose not." She looked as if it did, however. As if she suddenly realized that she didn't know whom she was dealing with. "Anyway, Georgette was nice enough. She changed, I think. I don't know. She told me that she and Pepper hadn't been together for a long time and that she was going to stay around here for a while. Really, that's all." Since I wasn't Livingston, her manner indicated, it might be best if I left.

"You loaned them your car, I understand."

"Yes, I did. That's all, though. And only until they could pick up one of their own."

"You also might have told Pepper where they were staying."

"Now wait a minute! If you think—"

"It's a possibility," I insisted. "He's in town. I met him. He was looking for them. It's hard to believe that if she could find you he couldn't. Or that if you were afraid of her you weren't even more afraid of him. So it's a very distinct possibility. I don't really care, however. All I care about is finding Steve. Have you seen him at any time during the past two days? Have you heard from him? Have you any idea where he could be?"

"No. I don't know where he is. I haven't heard from him. I swear I haven't." She was starting to come apart. Her eyes had widened, and so had her nostrils. "I don't know what Pablo told you about me but I don't know where Steve is. You can't believe everything Pablo says. He's got problems. That's why we're divorced. He's always had problems. You can't believe everything he says. I couldn't take it any longer. I thought I could but I couldn't. It was just too much for me."

"Couldn't take what?"

"His friends. Friends like Joey and Sol and Vincent. Especially that Goddamn Vincent Lee Remington. He followed Pablo here from California. Women I could understand, but men—" She uttered a sound of disgust.

I didn't know whether she was telling the truth or not. It was possible that she was. That would explain Pablo's reluctance to have dealings with the police. "I'm not interested in Pablo's problems or yours. All I'm interested in is where Steve is. Do you know anyone else he might try to get in touch with here in Chicago?"

"No!" Her voice had become shrill. "I don't know. I told you that. I don't know anything about him and I don't care anything about him. Now please leave. I don't even know who you are."

"I'm his father."

"Good for you. Now go."

There was nothing to be gained by staying. I put my glass down and went to the door. She followed me. She was breathing hard. "Thank you for the drink," I said, "and for your help."

She said nothing. And as soon as I was outside she closed the door with a bang. Put the safety chain on, too. I could hear the rattle.

Other than the fact that she was frightened I hadn't learned anything. And the fact that she was frightened wouldn't help me find Steve. Unless she did know where he was and that was what was frightening her.

I got into my car and drove around the block. I went past the house again, drove to the middle of the next block, pulled into a driveway and turned the car around. I crept along until I found a spot where I could watch without being visible. I parked there and waited. I wasn't certain that anything would happen but I thought that it might.

And it did. Almost immediately.

The garage door opened and a red MG backed down the driveway. Sally was at the wheel.

I let her get a block ahead, then started after her, keeping my distance. It was a quiet street, and the pursuit was easy. But then she turned onto Crawford Avenue, and the job became more difficult, because of the traffic. And because the MG suddenly began to weave back and forth between cars, as if Sally had discovered she was being followed.

I managed to keep up with her until we came to Dempster. There the light changed just as I reached the intersection. Sally had turned left. I went through the red light and turned left also.

There was a screech of brakes as a blue Cadillac skidded to a sudden stop, inches from my right fender. I jammed on my brakes too. I couldn't hear the driver of the other car but I could see him. He was shouting at me. He insisted on having the right of way and pulled his car around mine. By the time I got across the intersection the red MG was no longer in sight.

25

I hung my overcoat in the closet and went into the bedroom. I felt very tired. Not the weak, exhausted kind of tired I'd felt during the fevers. This was different. This was the kind of tired I'd felt in the past when I'd hoped for something and been disappointed.

There'd been a chance. Olive had pointed me toward Pablo. Pablo had pointed me toward Sally. Sally might have pointed me toward Steve—but I'd lost her. I hadn't lost her at the stoplight. I'd lost her when she realized that someone was following her. If she hadn't got away from me at that intersection she would have got away from me at another. Or led me back to her own house.

For a brief period I'd been hopeful, though. And now that hope was gone. Like so many other hopes. Perhaps it had been unrealistic to think that I could succeed where the FBI had so far failed. To believe that of all the seekers I'd be the finder. Nevertheless I was disappointed.

I turned on the five-thirty news. There was nothing about the search for Georgette's murderer. A member of the Senate Armed Services Committee who'd been interviewed on *Meet the Press* had had some unflattering things to say about a four-star general. A private plane carrying four persons to a ski resort had crashed into the side of a mountain; rescue efforts were being delayed by snow, but it was believed that all four persons were dead. There'd been a minor earthquake in Mexico—no deaths but considerable property damage. There'd been some good football games, too. The Rams and the Cowboys had won, as I'd predicted, but the Vikings had lost by thirteen points in one of the major upsets of the season.

After the news one of the outdoor shows came on. It dealt with a moose hunt in Canada. The purpose of the hunt was to put identification tags on the animals for future scientific studies. One big moose put up quite a struggle. He didn't know that he was being chased for purely scientific purposes and was pretty damn scared.

I turned the television set off. I wondered whether either the senator or the four-star general was a friend of Delmore Livingston's. I decided that both probably were. And I wondered whether Sally would have told me more if I'd let her go on thinking that I was Livingston. She might have. She certainly knew more than she'd revealed. She was afraid of something. She'd been worried that Pablo had mentioned it to me.

Poor Pablo. Caught in a three-way squeeze between Sally, Pepper and Vincent Lee Remington. Even with a profit of a hundred thousand a year he must have had some rough moments.

I looked around at the decor of my own apartment. It consisted mostly of pieces that Rita and I had picked up at resale shops and refinished ourselves. Rita had a talent for that sort of thing. Everyone who saw the place seemed to like it. I wished that Rita hadn't had to go to St. Louis. I missed her. And there was going to be so little time.

Depression swirled through the air and came closer. Real depression. The kind I'd experienced in the hospital. I tried to fend it off. It was liable to be a losing battle, I thought.

I remembered the prescription Fenwick had given me. It was still on the desk. I needed something and needed it now. I put the prescription in my pocket and got my overcoat from the closet. The drugstore on Clark had a pharmacist who worked on Sundays.

In the elevator I met Mrs. Finnegan and Rainbow. Mrs. Finnegan was a widow. She had the apartment directly above mine. Rainbow was her German Shepherd. I liked him and resented him at the same time—unlike some of the other tenants, who resented him without liking him. He barked a lot, and when he barked you could hear him all over the fifth, sixth and seventh floors. Mrs. Finnegan defended him to all the disgruntled. He was a good watchdog, and a woman who lived alone needed a good watchdog. Mrs. Moriarity agreed with her. Mrs. Moriarity and Mrs. Finnegan were sisters.

"Why, Mr. Jackson," she said, obviously pleased to see me.

"How are you, Mrs. Finnegan?"

Rainbow sniffed at my overcoat, recognized me as a neighbor and let me scratch his ear.

"We were just talking about you yesterday," Mrs. Finnegan said. "I understand someone broke into your apartment."

Mrs. Moriarity, I thought. It's probably all over the building by now. "I thought so," I said. "It's possible I was wrong."

"You should get a dog."

Rainbow licked my hand.

"Perhaps," I said.

We reached the ground floor. Rainbow bounded across the lobby to the heavy glass door that separated the lobby from the vestibule. I unlocked it for him, and he bounded across the vestibule too, barking excitedly. I opened the street door, and Mrs. Finnegan and I followed him onto the sidewalk. We strolled together toward the corner.

"It's getting warmer," Mrs. Finnegan said.

I started to reply, but the words never came out.

There was a driveway between our building and the one next

144

door. It led to the two service entrances. During the week there was usually a delivery truck in it and often a second delivery truck double-parked on the street, waiting its turn. Not today, however. Today there was a car parked in the driveway, and a man standing beside the car.

He and I recognized each other at the same moment. He was Pepper Himes.

I was too stunned to react. He wasn't. He reached into his pocket and pulled out a gun.

Mrs. Finnegan saw the gun too. She screamed.

Rainbow raced into the driveway, braced himself, then sprang.

Pepper fired.

Rainbow shrieked and fell dead.

I recovered and hurled myself at Pepper, twisting my body sideways and keeping it low, as I'd learned to do when blocking.

I heard the gun and felt the bullet at the same instant. There was pain in my right thigh, just below the buttock. I then felt my body collide with Pepper's. My shoulder caught him at the knees. He staggered and fell backward. The gun flew out of his hand.

Mrs. Finnegan screamed again. And kept screaming.

Pepper reached out for the gun. I did too. I was closer. My fingers sent it skidding under the car. He got up. I tried to get up also but was too slow. His foot connected with the side of my face. The blow knocked me onto the dead dog.

Mrs. Finnegan was still screaming as the engine began to roar and the car screeched out of the driveway. The sight of the oncoming car paralyzed her. She flew two feet into the air when the left front fender struck her hip.

The car turned right and disappeared.

I eased my body off the dog and got to my knees. I could feel the blood running down my leg.

It had all happened in less than a minute. There'd been no witnesses.

But in the next five minutes a large crowd collected.

26

"What time is it?" I asked.

"Ten o'clock?" Burr replied.

"Which hospital is this?"

"Augustana."

"How's the lady?" I couldn't think of her name.

"Mrs. Finnegan's still unconscious."

I'd been unconscious too. They'd given me a hypo. Everything was still fuzzy. "Am I all right?"

"More or less. A bullet went through your leg but it went through just below the surface of the skin. It didn't do any real damage. What happened?"

"He killed the dog."

Burr nodded. "Who did?"

I had to work at recalling the name. "The man from California. Pepper."

"How did it happen?"

Bit by bit I reconstructed the moments in the driveway. It took much longer to recount the incident than it had taken the

146

incident to happen. All the wrong things seemed important. Except for one. "You've got to pick up Sally," I said.

"Sally who?" Burr wanted to know.

I told him. I made an attempt to explain my visit to her. I couldn't remember everything, but I got the essential part across.

After a while he left. I didn't know whether he was leaving in order to pick up Sally Wayne or in order to do something else. I was very tired.

I fell asleep.

It was dark. I tried to figure out where a light switch might be. I sat up and swung my legs over the side of the bed. My right thigh was sore and stiff. My face didn't feel so good either.

I could walk, though. I found a light switch near the door. I flicked it.

My watch said four-thirty. Four-thirty in the morning, I thought. Which morning, though? I couldn't remember having had a meal in the hospital, so it was probably Monday morning. But I thought I'd better check. I opened the door and went into the corridor.

There was a chair beside the door. A policeman was sitting in it. We looked at each other. He seemed as surprised as I was.

"What day is this?" I asked.

"Monday," he said.

I went back into the room. Jesus, I thought, a policeman.

I studied myself in the mirror. I looked awful. I needed a shave. And the two sides of my face didn't match. The left side was whiter than usual, and the right was black and blue. For a moment I couldn't come up with an explanation. Then I remembered Pepper's kicking me as I tried to get up. I remembered falling on the dog. I remembered everything. And shuddered.

A nurse came into the room. She told me I shouldn't be out of bed.

I asked her how Mrs. Finnegan was. She hadn't heard of Mrs.

Finnegan. I told her to ask the policeman. She did. He hadn't heard of Mrs. Finnegan either. I should go back to bed, the nurse told me, and would I like a drink? I said I'd like a drink very much. A Scotch. She said she couldn't do anything about that. Then maybe some coffee, I suggested. She seemed skeptical about the coffee too but said she'd see.

I went back to bed, and the nurse left. She did find some coffee. She brought it in a styrofoam cup, steaming. It was very bad coffee. I sipped it gratefully, however. It cleared my head and made everything seem more real.

The various pieces of the day fell into place. The people. Livingston. Olive. Pablo Wayne. Sally. It was a good thing I hadn't succeeded in following Sally, I thought. I might have followed her right into Pepper's arms. I was just damn lucky that Mrs. Finnegan had decided to go out at the same time I had. Even luckier that she'd taken Rainbow with her. Otherwise Rainbow would still be alive and I'd be dead. Poor Mrs. Finnegan. She was going to miss that dog. If she pulled through.

I relived the moments in the driveway after the police came. I'd told them everything that had happened. This crazy man had started shooting at Mrs. Finnegan and me from the driveway. Then he'd hit Mrs. Finnegan with the car. They'd wanted a description. I'd given them one. I hadn't told them the man's name, however. It hadn't seemed to me that I should. I'd merely insisted that they get in touch with Mr. Edmund Burr of the FBI. Insisted and insisted and insisted. I'd still been insisting when they wheeled me into the emergency room at the hospital.

Not giving them Pepper's name seemed foolish now. The police probably knew everything. Or if they didn't they soon would. And it was better that way. But I was glad that Burr had come. He knew more than any of the rest of them. He knew that no matter how things turned out I wasn't going to live.

At five-thirty the hospital sounds became more pronounced. I was beginning to get used to hospital routine. And to dislike it with intensity. The cleaning attendants with their rotary floor-polishers. The discouraged-looking men who came around twice a day, selling newspapers. The dieticians with their printed menus—circle whether you want mashed potato or rice. Except for a few football injuries, and except for the months when they were reconstructing Steve's insides, I'd never had much to do with hospitals. I was profoundly thankful now that I hadn't. They weren't happy places. I resolved to get out of this one as soon as possible.

The nurse came around to take my pulse and my temperature. Another nurse came around to collect what she called my valuables. I hadn't been in a position to give them to anyone before, and I refused to give them to the nurse now. She warned me that the hospital wouldn't be responsible for them and left.

Things got worse when a round-faced intern with very long sideburns came into the room with his clipboard to take my medical history. I wouldn't give it to him. He thought I was kidding and attempted to humor me. I wasn't kidding and I wouldn't be humored. He too left.

Another man in a white jacket came in. He was a bit older than the intern and his expression was more grave. "I understand you don't want to talk to us," he said.

"That's right," I agreed.

"Is there any particular reason?"

"I simply don't want to. My medical history is my own personal concern."

He didn't take it too well. Especially when I said I wouldn't let him examine me. He went to consult higher authority.

The dietician brought a menu. I was wrong: it wasn't mashed potato or rice; it was baked potato or rice. I circled nothing.

The man I really wanted to see didn't appear. The man with the newspapers. Either it was an oversight or he was scared off by the guard at the door. The story wouldn't have made television but it probably would be in the newspaper.

An older man came into the room. He introduced himself as Dr. Innes. He wanted to know why I wouldn't give my medical history, why I wouldn't let myself be examined. I told him I was a Christian Scientist. He wasn't willing to accept that. Hospitals had certain rules, he explained. So did I, I replied. He began to enumerate the problems. He was still enumerating them when Burr walked in.

"Get this guy off my back," I said.

"What's the matter?" Burr asked.

"The patient won't cooperate," Innes said.

"The patient wants to go home," I said.

"He refuses to give us his medical history or let us examine him," Innes said.

"Let me talk to him," Burr said.

The doctor left the room.

"They're only trying to do their job, Walter," Burr said.

"I know that," I replied. "But there are only three people who know how things stand—a hematologist, my regular doctor and you. I want to keep it that way. And I don't want to be in a hospital, Ed. I'd rather be anywhere in the world at the moment than in a hospital."

"You're injured."

"Not that injured. And I want to find my son."

"Leave that to us."

"I want to help."

"We went to Mrs. Wayne's."

"Did you get her?"

"Nobody was there. But we located the ex-husband you told me about."

"Get me out of here, Ed."

It took a lot of doing, but in the end it was accomplished. Except that instead of taking me home Burr took me to FBI headquarters.

27

We stopped at my apartment on the way, however. So that I could shave and change clothes. The clothes I was wearing were all messed up with blood. Mine and the dog's.

Before we went into the building Burr took me over to the driveway. I showed him where and how everything had happened. He asked a few questions. I answered them. Then I asked what had happened to Pepper's gun.

"The police have it," he replied.

"At least you have the fingerprints," I said.

They had fingerprints all right, Burr said. It was a matter of identifying them.

"That shouldn't be difficult," I said.

"I don't know," he said. "His file is missing."

"His file?"

"From the Police Department."

I stared at him.

"Doyle and Carstairs flew to California this morning," he said, and added, "I'm on the case now too. Officially."

"But how could his file be missing?"

Burr shrugged. "Friends. But I believe we have duplicate prints in Washington."

We went up to my apartment. The newspaper was outside the door. I picked it up.

"It's not much of a story," Burr said.

We went into the apartment, and I read the article. Burr was right: it wasn't much of a story. An attack on a man and a woman in which neither of them had been killed and the assailant hadn't been identified. If the attack had taken place in slum neighborhood it wouldn't have been mentioned at all.

I shaved and changed clothes. I wanted to shower also but account of the bandage on my thigh I couldn't. "I owe you lunch," I told Burr. "Would you like to collect?"

He said he wouldn't mind.

We went down the street to a place that had recently opened. P.K.'s, it was called. It was a fancy hamburger joint with oil paintings, Tiffany lampshades and a big salad bar. Burr liked it. I liked it too but I would have liked it better if the chair had been more comfortable. I realized that I'd have to avoid sitting on hard chairs for a while.

I tried to talk Burr out of making me go down to the office with him, but he was adamant. He wanted a detailed signed statement from me. He also wanted me to look at a picture of Pepper which a police artist had drawn from Pablo Wayne's description.

"What would you do this afternoon if you didn't come with me?" he asked.

"Stay home and wait for Steve to call," I replied. "I'm very very worried about him, Ed. I really am."

"We're doing everything we can, Walter. You know that."

I sighed.

"We've been checking all automobile sales for the past two weeks. We found where they bought the car. Now it's simply a question of locating it. There can't be that many black Fairlanes being driven around the city with no license plates."

"It's a big city, Ed. And he may even have gone somewhere else. New York. Anywhere."

"Besides, I don't like the idea of your sitting around that apartment alone. It isn't safe for you. I'm almost tempted to take you into protective custody. For your own good."

That sounded ominous. "I wouldn't be so keen on that. Pepper's taken his shot at me. He won't try again. At least not so soon. It wouldn't be safe for him. And if worse comes to worst I can stay at Rita's. She's still in St. Louis."

"That might not be such a bad idea. I'd feel better if you would."

"But if Steve calls—"

"I don't suppose you know how much money he had on him."

"No. Not very much, I think."

"So it isn't likely he's left the city." He changed the subject. "If you want to do something useful, get Livingston off our back."

"Ha," I said.

Calls had come in from half a dozen people in Washington, Burr said. What Livingston didn't realize was that he was accomplishing nothing other than creating more interest in the case than was healthy. Reporters had already started sniffing around, and such matters were handled more effectively when there was no publicity. If the case was aired by one of the network news commentators or written up in one of the national news magazines, every member of the jewel ring would be alerted.

"Don't you think they are already?" I asked.

"I don't know," Burr replied. "I'm inclined to think that they may not be. Pepper may be in a squeeze between the law and his own gang."

"He killed Georgette to protect the gang."

"Perhaps. But mainly to protect himself, I think."

"They wanted him to kill her."

"I'm not so sure about that. She was valuable to them. Women who can do what she did are hard to find, especially ones who have the opportunities she did. It's possible that all they wanted was for him to get her out of the way for a while. She may have made the mistake of threatening him. I'm inclined to believe that that was what happened."

"Steve didn't say anything about that."

"He may not have known. At any rate, Pepper has something to worry about. If the Syndicate decides—"

"The Syndicate?"

"Any large-scale theft ring has to have connections with the Syndicate. It doesn't matter whether it's cars or liquor or whatever. Small-time theft is one thing. Large-scale theft is something else again. A big ring simply can't operate on its own. It requires too many people, too many outlets, too much protection."

"Police protection?"

"Sometimes. Unfortunately. And lawyers and judges and— you name it. Pepper's all right as long as he doesn't get caught. But if he does get caught there's the possibility that he'll talk— just as there was that possibility with Georgette. Except that he probably knows a damn sight more than she did. So his buddies may not want to take any chances, especially if they think he's being hunted for murder. That's why he's so desperate, I think." He paused. "I wish you'd paid more attention to that car or got the license number."

"That's the last thing I had on my mind. I was too busy trying to keep from getting killed."

He permitted himself to smile. "I know. But I wish you had."

I tried to smile too, just to show my good intentions. But smiling, I found, hurt almost as much as sitting did.

He speared a cherry tomato with his fork. "Getting back to Livingston, though, what he also doesn't realize is that there's only so much we can do, no matter who gets on our tail. Have you any idea how many cases the Bureau is working on at the same time? Or even how many this office is working on? And all of them are important or we wouldn't have got them. This is one of the less important ones, actually. There's a shipment

154

of heroin supposedly coming in—" He broke off. "Well, anyway."

I read between the lines. I didn't like the message. On the one hand, don't worry about Steve: we'll find him and we'll also find Pepper. On the other hand, we can only give this case so much time and effort. There was a contradiction in that.

"Greed," Burr said sadly. "Plain human greed."

"I know," I said. I really didn't, but I remembered something that had happened years before, shortly after Rita and I had met. We were out one night, walking down Oak Street, when suddenly a kid snatched her pocketbook. I chased him, but he ducked into an alley and got away. We called the police. They asked us to come down to the station and look at mug shots of known purse-snatchers. We couldn't identify the one who'd snatched Rita's purse, but in the course of the evening at the police station I became friendly with the detective we were dealing with. I asked him, as a matter of curiosity, what was responsible for most crimes. I expected a different answer from the one I got. "Greed," the detective said. "Just greed."

"An easy buck," Burr went on. "Some guy thinks he's found the way. Then one thing leads to another, and pretty soon you have a murder case on your hands. It doesn't matter whether it's a Georgette or a Mrs. Finnegan or even a poor German Shepherd who's doing what he was bred to do—protect. Someone gets cornered and gets desperate and starts killing." He pushed his plate away and lit a cigar. "This is a nice place. I'll have to remember it."

It took me a long time to make the statement. It took an even longer time for the stenographer to type it.

While she was typing I studied the portrait of Pepper Himes which had been drawn by the artist. I didn't think that it was accurate in all respects. That created problems too. The artist didn't have his office in the building and had to be sent for. He didn't arrive right away. When he did arrive and I began to work with him he exaggerated my corrections. It took more

155

than thirty minutes for him to achieve what I thought was a true likeness of the man who'd come to my apartment to question me about Steve and who'd almost succeeded in killing me.

But when he did achieve it, it was a fine job. Seeing the picture was almost like seeing the man himself. And filled me with the same cold fear. "That's him, all right," I said.

Burr gazed at the picture over my shoulder, and as he did I recalled his words: cornered, desperate. The artist had captured some of that, it seemed to me—as a result of my corrections. That was the difference between the man I remembered and the man Pablo remembered: desperation.

The stenographer returned with my statement. I read it over, shifted my weight gingerly on the chair and signed my name.

"Now what?" I asked Burr.

"Now take a taxi to Rita's apartment and stay there."

"For how long?"

He picked up the artist's sketch. "Until we find this guy." He squinted at it as if trying to analyze the mind behind the face. "If only we knew more about him—where he'd be most likely to go, whom he'd be most likely to meet."

"Sally Wayne could tell you," I said.

"Except that now we can't find her either, thanks to you. If only you'd told us about her and let us handle it." He shook his head. "I still have half a mind to take you into protective custody."

"That wouldn't do you any good."

"It would keep you from maybe getting shot at again. And now you're more important to us than ever."

"I am?"

"You are. Because when we nail Pepper Himes even if we can't pin anything else on him we can stick him with an attempted-murder charge. He tried to kill you. You could testify to that in court."

I hadn't thought of that. I thought of it now, though. "I suppose I could," I said. "When would the trial take place?"

"Who knows? By the time we gather all the evidence and the

156

State prepares its case and gets a court date—six months, maybe, a year."

"By then I won't be around, Ed."

He looked at me. His expression softened. "I forgot about that." He took a deep breath. His expression hardened again. "Well, you may know it, and I may know it, but Pepper Himes doesn't know it."

That, I thought, was quite true.

But Burr didn't say anything further about protective custody.

28

Walking wasn't a comfortable exercise at the moment, but I walked anyway. At first because it was the rush hour and I couldn't get a taxi. Then because I found that the air was nice and it was pleasant to be caught up in the crowd of homeward-bound office workers and holiday shoppers.

It was slightly over a mile from the Federal Building to the Wrigley Building. I walked all the way, stopping only once—to look at the display in the window of the American Express office on Michigan Avenue. The display featured some nice pictures of Jamaica. I gazed wistfully at them for a few moments, seeing myself, in good health and free of problems, stretched out on the beach with Rita beside me. Then I continued my walk.

The same bartender was on duty. Harry. He was very busy, however. All of the bar stools were occupied, and there were people standing two deep behind the stools. I had to squeeze between two portly gentlemen with scarves around their necks, just to place my order.

Harry recognized me, though. He smiled. His smile faded.

"What happened to your face?" he asked.

"I fell down in a driveway," I replied.

He clucked sympathetically. "Martini?"

"Scotch today. On the rocks."

He poured the drink. I glanced at the people around me. I didn't see Franken. I wondered whether he was still romancing Garrison. The men flanking me weren't the only ones with scarves, I noted. Evidently that was the thing this season. Remove your overcoat but keep your scarf on your shoulders. I had an agreeable feeling of anonymity. There wasn't a soul in the place that I knew. Advertising executives had always been outside my realm, and judging by the fragments of conversation I was picking up, that was what most of these people were. Advertising or communications of some sort. The words I caught were "audience," "survey," "concept" and "identification." "Identification" seemed to have something to do with the shape of a box.

I put five dollars on the bar. Harry took it and gave me change.

"Where's Mr. Franken?" I asked.

"You heard?" he replied.

"Heard what?"

"I just heard about it myself this noon. Mr. Wickes told me."

"Told you what?"

"Then you didn't hear. They took Mr. Franken to the hospital yesterday. He passed out. Bleeding ulcer, Mr. Wickes said. Been bleeding right along, I guess." He wiped some moisture from the base of my glass. "Man like that—he shouldn't drink."

I nodded. Every drama had its third act. All you had to do was stick around. I felt sorry for Franken, somehow. "There's all kinds of desperation," I said.

"People are their own worst enemies," Harry said.

I moved to a less congested spot. And tried to imagine that I was Pepper Himes:

I've killed my wife. On the second try. The first try didn't work, because this kid she was shacked up with got in the way.

He saw me make the attempt, though.

My imagination stopped right there. Steve was a threat to Pepper for that one incident alone.

I tried to imagine that I was Steve:

I know the man's a killer. I know he knows I know it. I'm afraid to go to the police, because they'll probably think I was part of the jewel ring and may even think that I killed Georgette, and even if they don't think either of those things, they know I passed a bad check. Both of my fathers want to turn me in, although for different reasons. I have a car but very little money, no friends in town, only the clothes on my back. What should I do?

My imagination stopped there also. I simply didn't know what I'd do in a situation like that. Caught between fear of Pepper and fear of the law, I'd try to make myself as inconspicuous as possible. I'd need money in order to do that, though. Where would I get money? Would I try to pass another bad check or would I be afraid to?

No telling.

I finished my drink and went to the apartment. My apartment, not Rita's. In spite of Burr and in spite of Pepper.

Steve couldn't trust anyone completely. But he'd be more likely to trust me than to trust anyone else.

No one shot me as I walked into the living room. The place was exactly as I'd left it. I fixed myself something to eat and began to plan what I'd do if Steve called.

I thought of Ben Small.

I thought of Jack Kinney. I hadn't thought of Jack Kinney in years. I'd blocked him out of my mind. But now I found myself wondering whether he still remembered me.

29

All things considered, it wasn't a bad evening. Alone in my apartment, surrounded by familiar objects, I pulled myself together. I began to feel that I was still myself. That while I might not have a long future I still had *some* future and that what I did with it was within *my* control. Not Pepper's. Not Burr's. Not even Steve's. Mine.

What I intended to do, though, did depend upon Steve. Upon my being able to reach him. Once contact was established, I could use whatever time and energy I had left to redirect his life. It needed it.

Actually, he wasn't in as much of a jam as he thought he was. The only crime he'd committed was passing bad checks, and since Livingston had made the checks good there were no criminal charges against him. If it should turn out that there were any checks which Livingston hadn't made good I could come up with the money myself.

Steve would have to straighten himself out with the police in regard to Georgette's murder. To prove that he was somewhere else at the time. That shouldn't be difficult. He'd also have to tell the FBI everything he knew about Georgette's activities. But when those two duties had been carried out he'd be free. All he'd have to worry about then was Pepper.

And Pepper would eventually be caught. It was simply a matter of finding a safe place for Steve in the meanwhile. But that shouldn't be a problem. The world was a big place.

The main thing was not to let him go back to California, to the environment that had got him into trouble in the first place. Now that he was away from his mother and Livingston he had to stay away. What he needed most was a job, and I could help him there. Ben Small would find something for him. Or Charly Kipness.

But first I had to get in touch with him. He had to call me.

And he would. Because he had no one else to turn to.

It was a fine group he'd fallen in with. The woman he was living with was working with her estranged husband, who in addition to being a crook was evidently involved with her former girlfriend, who was married to their boss, who was bisexual. A great little circle.

I jumped when the telephone rang.

It wasn't Steve, though. It was Rita. She was frantic. She'd been calling every hospital in the city. How was I, and what had happened?

I was a little banged up, I said. I'd had a slight run-in with Pepper Himes. But I was getting over it.

"Thank God!"

"How did you find out, honey?"

"Julie talked to Terry. He'd seen it in the paper. Julie called me."

Good old Terry. Always on top of things. "A lot has happened, honey. Not much of it good. Steve's disappeared. Livingston and my ex-wife are in town. The police and the FBI are looking for Pepper and for Steve but they haven't found either one of them, and Livingston's throwing his weight around with everyone up to and probably including the President of the United States."

"I'm coming home."

"Please don't, honey. Not on my account. You can't help. There isn't even much that I can do myself. I've just been sitting here, hoping that Steve would come to his senses and let me try to help him. It's nothing more than a waiting game at the moment. And down there you can do something useful."

"I don't know. The doctor is pretty sure that Ann isn't going to lose the baby."

"She's pregnant and she has a broken leg. She needs someone to help her."

"Nils can cook. He's a better cook than I am."

We went around and around about it, with me trying to talk her out of what I really wanted her to do and Rita trying to persuade me that she should. We came to no conclusion. But we talked for thirty minutes, and I told her what had been going on. It was a relief to unburden myself, and I felt better at the end of the half-hour than I'd felt before. She promised to call me again in the morning.

Shortly after I finished talking to Rita, Charly Kipness called. He hadn't seen the item about me in the newspaper but he'd noticed that my office was dark all day and wanted to know if things were OK. I told him that I'd had a slight accident. He suggested that he come over. I started to say no but thought better of it. I could broach the subject of his taking Steve in with him.

"I'd welcome a little company," I said.

"I'll be there in twenty minutes," he said eagerly.

And he was. A change had come over him. He'd got a haircut and was wearing a tie I'd never seen before. But those were incidentals. It was his manner that was the most different. The way he talked, the way he moved. There was a brightness in his eyes, an assurance in his voice, a spring in his step which I'd noticed before only when he was telling me about a particularly good round of golf.

He was taken aback by the alteration in my appearance. My bruised face, the care I took in sitting down, the stiffness with which I walked. I explained that this nut had tried to kill one of the neighbors and myself and that I'd acquired my wounds in the scuffle. He was shocked.

What he really wanted to discuss, however, was my plan to turn my business over to him. I elaborated on it and sounded him out about Steve. Ideally, I said, Ben Small would let him keep the Carling-Small business, and Steve could service the account. Ben was in Florida at the moment, but I intended to speak to him as soon as I could. If he should say no—well, what would Charly's feelings be then?

Charly's feelings appeared to be on the positive side. He wanted to know all about Steve. Actually, I said, I didn't know Steve that well. I'd hardly seen him since he was a baby. But he'd recently come back into my life and he seemed to be a nice young man. He was rather at loose ends at the moment, but I thought he'd be good in the insurance business once he learned something about it. As soon as I could I'd introduce them. The three of us would have lunch together.

That was fine with Charly. But what about me? he asked. I had a yen to spend my declining days in California, I said.

"You're too young to talk about declining days, Walter."

"Not really, friend."

"By the way, did you get hold of that beautician yesterday?"

"Yes."

"What about Rita? Will she go to California with you?"

"I don't know. She's in St. Louis at the moment. Her older daughter had an accident."

"Sorry to hear it."

All in all, it was about as satisfactory a conversation as we could have under the circumstances. And I made a mental note to set up an appointment with Ben.

It was after eleven when Charly left. I was disappointed that

I hadn't heard from Steve but reminded myself that I'd just have to be patient. He probably hadn't run out of money yet or grasped the fact that I was his best bet.

I poured myself a pony of cognac and drank it as I was getting undressed. Then I got into bed. The day had been a mighty long one. I wondered what they'd written on my record at the hospital. I wondered about Mrs. Finnegan. I'd have to talk to Mrs. Moriarity in the morning. I turned out the light.

The telephone rang.

I grabbed it. "Hello."

There was no voice at the other end.

"Hello. Hello. Who is it? Is it you, Steve?"

The party at the other end hung up.

I turned on the light. Something began to jump around inside of me. Had it been Steve? Had he wanted to talk to me and then lost his nerve?

I recalled the last time. It hadn't been Steve. It had been Pepper, checking to make sure I was home. The telephone call had been followed within minutes by a visit.

He'd broken into the apartment once. He could do it again.

I got out of bed and dressed as quickly as I could. Burr was right. My apartment wasn't safe.

In less than five minutes I was in the elevator. I pushed "G" and rode down to the garage. The garage was in the basement.

The garage attendant was sound asleep in the front seat of a Mercury. I hurried over to my car. It was in its usual stall. I opened front and rear doors. Everything was all right.

My heart was still pounding when I arrived at Rita's. I let myself in and after a while I went to bed. I couldn't fall asleep, though. I kept seeing Pepper poking around in my apartment. Would he wait there for me to return? The image of the real Pepper was followed by an image of the artist's sketch of him. In some ways the sketch was even more menacing.

I'd have to call Burr in the morning.

What did protective custody really mean? I wondered. Where did they put you when they put you in protective custody? Maybe they didn't put you anyplace. Maybe they just stationed a policeman outside your door, as they'd done at the hospital.

Whatever they did, I wouldn't like it.

I had to be careful, though. Pepper wasn't about to give up.

It was almost dawn before I fell asleep. And when I did I had a nightmare. I dreamed that Pepper was in a room with me, looking at the sketch of himself. He put the sketch down and turned to me. He had a gun in his hand.

I woke up.

I thought I heard a footstep.

I did hear a footstep. But it was in the apartment upstairs.

30

Without Rita the apartment seemed strange. I felt like a trespasser. I made the bed and left as soon as I could.

I drove to my office. I could call Burr from there. Furthermore, if I didn't start paying some attention to business there wouldn't be anything left to turn over to Charly.

The cleaning woman had stacked my mail on the desk. There was quite a bit of it, including a note from the public stenographer. Would I please pick up the letters she'd typed for me? At the bottom of the note she'd written, "$2.75."

I called Burr. He was out. I started to ask for Doyle or Carstairs but remembered that they were in California. I left my name and number.

I looked across the air shaft. Charly was in his office. He was writing something. He put the pen down and picked up the telephone. Then he swung his chair around and saw me. I waved. With his free hand he indicated someone drinking a cup of coffee. I made a circle with my thumb and forefinger.

He finished his telephone call and put on his jacket. I left my office. I took the stenographer's note with me. Charly and I met at the elevator.

He inspected my face. "You sure must have got a whack," he said.

"It'll take a while for the color to go away. Remind me to stop at the public stenographer's on the way back. I have to pick up some stuff she did for me."

Mr. Anderson joined us. He was one of the partners of Anderson, Atkins, Allen and Smith. They occupied almost one entire side of the floor. They were the third-largest insurance brokerage firm in the city. At one time I'd thought I might apply to them for a job but I'd decided against it. Better to be my own boss. Anderson too inspected my face. Then he remembered he'd seen something about me in the newspaper.

I told him what I'd told Charly.

"Ah, yes," he said, and at that moment the elevator came.

There were several coffee shops on the ground floor. All of them were crowded. We had to stand in line.

"How'd you like to have a business like Anderson, Atkins, Allen and Smith?" Charly asked me. "Wouldn't that be something?"

"There's no harm in thinking big," I admitted.

"They weren't always big. They started the same as everybody else."

"True." Painful as it was, I smiled. It was nice to know that Charly had acquired aspirations. For a moment I shared his fantasy. I saw him and Steve at the head of a large firm with a lot of junior partners. Anything was possible.

The hostess seated us.

Having started a fantasy, Charly was reluctant to give it up. Over coffee and a doughnut he named a number of the city's leading manufacturers and speculated on what it would take to get some of their business. Reputation, he decided. The big people want to go where the other big people are. An account like Carling-Small could be used as a magnet to attract other corporations of the same size.

168

"How come you never went after them, Walter?" he asked.

"I was asking myself that question just the other day," I replied. "I don't know. I did. I still do, occasionally. I didn't have what it takes, I guess. I didn't have the will."

"You played football, though."

"So?"

"That takes will."

"That was different."

He let the matter drop. I glanced at the men at the next table. There were two of them. Both were letting their coffee get cold while they read newspapers.

Charly brought up the subject of his friend Larry, the one in the beauticians'-supply business. Even the beauty shops were becoming big, Larry had told him. Many of them were actually part of chains. They operated under different names, but the same people owned them all.

"It's a damn profitable business, Larry says. A lot of headaches, though. The operators, if they're any good, all have their own clientele, and they're more temperamental than actors. If they don't like the way you look at them they quit—and take their customers with them."

"Insurance people do the same thing."

"We're not as temperamental, though."

One of the men at the next table put his newspaper down, glanced at his watch and gulped his coffee. "We're going to be late," he said to his friend. The friend put his newspaper down and glanced at his watch too. Then he gulped his coffee, and they got up. The first one left his newspaper on the table.

I wondered whether there was anything further in the paper about Georgette. I reached over and took the one that had been left behind.

It was open at the stock-market page. I looked at the listing for Carling-Small. That was the only stock I followed with any regularity. I owned a hundred shares.

Fifty-three and an eighth. It had dropped one-eighth the day before.

I folded the paper back to its original order, with page one on top. The headline said, TEACHERS REFUSE COMPROMISE.

Then, for several moments, my heart seemed to stop.

Next to the article about the teachers was another one. The headline for that one said, MILLIONAIRE'S SON HELD IN SLAYING.

Steve had been arrested.

31

I didn't actually go crazy but I did behave irrationally. I got into my car and drove to the Town Hall police station, on North Halsted Street. That made no sense whatsoever. I didn't know whether Steve had been arrested in that district or not. All I knew was that he'd been arrested somewhere on Western Avenue, trying to sell his car back to the dealer he'd bought it from. But the Town Hall station was the first one that came to mind, because I'd once lived near it. So I raced from downtown up to the mid-north side, ran inside like a maniac and approached one policeman after another, explaining incoherently that I was looking for my son.

The reactions I got varied. One policeman thought that I was trying to locate a lost child. Another, noticing the bruises on my face, had the idea that my son had beat me up. A third, for some reason, believed that I was the victim of a hit-and-run driver. I kept trying to tell them that my son hadn't killed anybody and that if they didn't believe me they could call the FBI. Finally I called the FBI myself. Mr. Burr was still out, I was told; would

I leave my name? Oh, yes, Mr. Jackson—they already had one message from me.

The frustration only made me more agitated. Instead of sitting down for a few minutes and working things out logically, I ran back to my car and drove to the only other police station I could think of on the spur of the moment, the Chicago Avenue station. My behavior there wasn't much different from what it had been at the Town Hall station, except that I further confused the issue by stating that a Los Angeles policeman was trying to kill my son and the FBI had to be informed. Several of the officers gathered around me and made an attempt to get a straight story, but just as we were at the point of a breakthrough someone came in wanting to know who'd left a car in the no-parking zone in front of the building. I said that I had and that this was an emergency and that I was a taxpayer, and the situation deteriorated again.

In the end they made me move my car, which was a good thing, because the simple matter of finding a parking space settled me down. I began to realize that I was acting like a nut and to try to figure out how to make myself understood. I'd left the first newspaper in the coffee shop but on my way back to the police station I bought a second one. Armed with that, I was able to identify myself and my problem. Even then it was difficult, for they wanted to know why my name wasn't Livingston, and I had to go into the story of my divorce and Steve's adoption. But finally a helpful plainclothesman assured me that Steve wasn't being held at the Chicago Avenue station and suggested that I make my inquiries at police headquarters, at Eleventh and State.

"I should have thought of that in the first place," I said.

So many anxieties were at work on me, however, that although I knew where to go I didn't go there. Driving down Clark Street on my way to police headquarters, I suddenly decided that I was making a mistake by bothering with the police at all. The place to go was the FBI office. If Burr wasn't there someone else would be.

The receptionist knew who I was. She asked me how I was feeling. I said I was feeling better and that I had to see Mr. Burr —Steve had been arrested. She said she didn't know anything about that; Mr. Burr was out, and she didn't have any idea when he'd be back, but if I wanted to wait I was welcome to. I asked to talk to someone else. She called for a Mr. Glenn, who came to the reception room and explained that this wasn't his case and that the thing for me to do was wait for Burr.

I waited twenty minutes. Burr didn't return. I left.

So after three hours of illogical and fruitless activity I arrived at police headquarters, where I spent another hour and a half.

The problem there wasn't one of communication; it was one of authority. I was directed from one office to another. At each I had to wait, because the man I was supposed to see was busy. At each I had to explain what I wanted. At each I was told that I'd have to see someone who had "the authority."

It wasn't until a quarter past two that I finally got to a Captain Daniels, who did have the authority and who, with one simple telephone call, obtained the information I wanted.

Steve Livingston had been taken to Area Six, Captain Daniels said. Area Six was on North Damon Avenue.

As I drove up to the building I saw Steve being led away. Three men were with him. Two of them I didn't recognize, the third I did. Oscar Owen Nelson. They got into an unmarked car and drove away. In order to follow them I had to turn around. By the time I found an alley and got my car pointed the right way, the car with Steve in it had disappeared.

My anxiety eased, however. Evidently Steve had managed to get in touch with Livingston, and Livingston had called the lawyer. Steve was in good hands.

I went into the building. I explained to the officer at the desk that I wanted to find out about Steve Livingston. He seemed not to have heard of him.

"You've just been questioning him," I said.

"About what?" he asked.

"A murder," I said.

"Upstairs," he told me.

I climbed the narrow steps to the second floor. A sign said, CRIMINAL INVESTIGATION. I went through the doorway. A number of men were in the room. All of them were talking on telephones. I waited and studied the bulletin board. It was crowded with mug shots of purse-snatchers. For a moment I thought of the detective I'd become acquainted with when Rita's purse had been snatched.

Greed. Just greed.

Tacked to the wall next to the bulletin board was an announcement for a retirement party for Investigator Pat Larkin. Cocktails at 6:30, dinner at 7:30, ladies invited.

One of the plainclothesmen finished his call. I approached him. He hadn't heard of Steve either. "What'd he do?" he wanted to know.

"He didn't do anything," I said. "But you were questioning him about a murder."

"Upstairs," he said.

And on the third floor I found myself in the right place. MURDER, SEX AND AGGRAVATED ASSAULT, the sign said. With a red crayon someone had underlined SEX. Another sign asked, *Does Your Appearance Command Respect?* I smoothed my hair and stated my problem to the first man I saw with a gun. He referred me to Lieutenant Vine.

Lieutenant Vine looked very tired. He had a bottle of Bufferin tablets on his desk. Also a coffee mug. The coffee mug needed washing.

Lieutenant Vine refused to tell me anything. He refused even to believe that I was Steve's father. I told him to check with the FBI. He told me to check with the FBI myself. I did. Mr. Burr had returned, the operator told me, but was not available. As far as Lieutenant Vine was concerned, that ended things. He was off duty and he was going home. He'd been working for eighteen hours and had a headache.

No one else would tell me anything either.

I drove back to the FBI office. Mr. Burr was still unavailable.

I sat in the reception room until a quarter to five, at which time I saw Oscar Owen Nelson come out of one of the inner offices. I grabbed his arm.

"Is Steve here?" I asked.

He nodded.

"What's happening?"

"They're questioning him." Nelson detached himself from my grip and went outside to the corridor. I followed him. He headed toward the men's room. Just before he went inside he said, "It won't do you any good to wait around. They won't let you see him."

"How long is it going to take?" I asked.

"Who knows?" he replied. "They're just getting started."

Nevertheless I waited some more.

Finally Burr came through the reception room. "What are you doing here?" he asked.

"I want to see Steve," I said.

He shook his head. "You can't. Go home. I'll talk to you tomorrow."

"Is he all right?"

He shrugged. And he too went to the men's room.

At nine o'clock I gave up and went back to Rita's.

Rita had come home.

32

It was the news of Steve's arrest that had brought her
back. The story had been in the newspapers even in St. Louis.
And upon her return she'd seen an item about it on television.
So she knew more of what was going on than I did.

The television program had been a local one rather than
national. The commentator had referred to Steve as "the traveling companion of Mrs. Georgette Himes, the Los Angeles
woman who was found shot to death last Friday in a motel on
the city's northwest side." Also as "the son of California millionaire Delmore Livingston." Georgette, the commentator
said, "was believed by police to be linked with a ring of jewel
thieves operating on the West Coast." There'd been no film
with the report and no mention of Steve's having been charged
with the crime. It had said merely that he was being questioned.

Rita and I tried to draw some conclusions. The fact that Steve
had been in custody for twenty-four hours meant that the police
had had time to check his alibi. The fact that they'd turned him
over to the FBI might or might not mean that the police were

finished with him. But I recalled that he hadn't been hand-cuffed when I'd seen him leaving the police station.

Rita believed that Steve would soon be released. I was half inclined to agree with her. But what worried me was his safety. What steps would be taken to protect him after his release?

"As long as he's in the FBI office he's safe," Rita said. "And they'll figure out some way to keep him safe after he leaves."

I tried to share her optimism.

Then, in the midst of everything, with both of us tired and distracted, she announced that she'd decided to marry me.

I was so nonplused by the statement, so unprepared for it, that, having made it, she began to apologize.

"I know this is the wrong time," she said. "I didn't intend to say anything just yet. I planned it all different. Something nice and romantic. I don't know why I brought it up now. I'm sorry."

I simply couldn't think of anything to say.

"You still want to, don't you?" Rita asked.

I couldn't even nod.

"I know what I always said," she went on, looking flushed and uncomfortable, "but when I was down in St. Louis I began to think. I mean, Ann and Nils—they seem so happy. And I began to think about Julie. To all extents and purposes she's on her own now. She's going to have a good life—I just know it. The only ones whose futures are kind of up in the air are you and me. We've been half together and half apart for so long that we've come to take it for granted, or at least I have. But are we being fair to ourselves? I used to think—to hope—that Joe, that someday . . . But I've just been kidding myself. I know that. I guess I've known it for some time now."

Faced with my silence, she seemed to feel that she had to keep talking. She began to ramble. First about Julie. She didn't think that Julie was serious about Terry. Even if she was, though, it wouldn't be so terrible—Terry was really nicer than I thought he was. Then about my not driving her to the airport. She'd been angry about that, and now that she knew why I'd refused she felt guilty. The thing was, she'd sensed immediately that Steve had something to do with my refusal and she'd felt a sort of jealousy, and now she felt guilty about that too. And finally about Ann and Nils and what a nice couple they were.

I wanted to take her in my arms. I wanted to tell her that I loved her. I wanted to tell her that I was going to die.

I couldn't. I was afraid of what it would be like after I did.

Finally I said, "Stop, darling. Please. Let's talk about it later. This isn't the time."

She stopped. She looked very hurt, though.

"I'll fix us a drink," I said.

"I don't think I want a drink," she replied.

I'd intended to spend the night. But now it didn't seem to me that I could. "I think I'd better be getting back to the FBI office," I said. I hadn't planned to go back to the FBI office. It was the only thing I could think of to say, however.

Rita nodded. And let me leave.

I walked around for a few minutes. I didn't quite know where to go. Finally I got into my car and drove over to the place where Burr and I had had lunch, P.K.'s. The restaurant part was crowded, but the bar wasn't. I went to the bar.

For the first time in almost two weeks I had no thoughts of Steve or of the FBI or of the police. Pepper Himes, as far as I was concerned, had ceased to exist. Georgette, Pablo, Sally suddenly meant nothing to me. They were part of a troubled and frightening little charade that I'd also been part of for a few days but which was outside the mainstream of my life.

Rita was in the mainstream of my life. The years of closeness we'd shared, which had followed the barren years before, which had followed the years with Olive, which had followed my adolescence and childhood. There had been a current of people and events, and Rita had been important in it. Actually, I reflected, I'd spent more years with her than I'd spent with Olive.

Now the current was about to stop. Two months, three months. Soon. More than anything else in the world I wanted it to continue. But it wasn't going to.

I tried to recapture the feeling I'd had the night before. My life wasn't over yet. I still had *some* future. What future I had was within my control. The feeling wouldn't come back, however. The future was not within my control. No way. I couldn't marry Rita even if I thought it was wise. There wouldn't be enough time to see her through her divorce proceedings.

So perhaps the thing to do was break with her now. Then just go away and live out my little future free of the weight of caring and being cared about. For what would it be like if I didn't? Misunderstanding and strain, deceit and regret.

Did I have enough guts to do it? To go away and stay away? To die among strangers?

I didn't know.

Or would it be better to tell Rita the truth? To impose upon her the burden of watching the days and hours slip by?

I didn't know that either.

There were so many things that might have been. So few of them would now come to pass. Whatever had already happened in my life—that was what I was stuck with. There wouldn't be much of a chance to correct mistakes.

I finished my drink and ordered another. Then I found a table and ordered something to eat.

It was after eleven when I left P.K.'s. I drove home and put my car in the garage. I stopped in the vestibule to pick up my mail. A bill from the hematologist, my alumni bulletin and a folded-up note from Mrs. Moriarity. The note said, "Please see me. *Important!*"

I glanced at my watch. She might be asleep. On the other hand, she'd said "Important."

I went up to her apartment and rang the bell.

"Who is it?" she called through the closed door.

I told her.

The door swung open to reveal Mrs. Moriarity in felt slippers and a kimono, looking wan. I must have looked worse to her, though, than she looked to me, for when she saw me she drew back and exclaimed, "Oh, my! Should you be out of the hospital?"

"I'm all right," I said. "How's Mrs. Finnegan?"

She said that Mrs. Finnegan had regained consciousness and that the doctors offered encouragement.

"I got your note," I said.

She invited me in. Then she closed the door and lowered her voice. "I looked for you in the hospital yesterday, but they said you'd gone. I wanted to tell you about the man."

"What man?" I asked.

"The man in your apartment. Was it all right for him to be there?"

"I don't know what you're talking about," I said.

"There was a man in your apartment yesterday. Mr. Rowe saw him coming out." Mr. Rowe was my next-door neighbor.

I got that cold feeling at the base of my spine.

"I didn't know whether to call the police or not. I mean, since Mr. Rowe saw him leaving I didn't think there was any point. But after what happened on Sunday—"

"What did the man look like?"

Mrs. Moriarity gave me, second-hand, the description which Mr. Rowe had given her. It was so general that I couldn't determine whether it was Pepper who'd been in my apartment or not. I was inclined to believe that it was, however.

"No," I said. "It wasn't all right."

The corners of her mouth turned down. "I don't know, Mr. Jackson. People in your apartment who shouldn't be there. The man who shot you, who hit my sister with the car—"

"I agree with you, Mrs. Moriarity," I said quickly. "There are a lot of dangerous people around."

"I try to run a good building. If there's something going on that isn't right, I'll have to speak to the owners."

"You certainly should, Mrs. Moriarity. And I appreciate your telling me about the man Mr. Rowe saw. Next time call the police." I backed toward the door.

Mrs. Moriarity still appeared to be skeptical.

"By all means," I added, and left.

I decided not to spend the night in my apartment. I went to the Holiday Inn on Lake Shore Drive instead. For I realized that while the charade might be outside the mainstream of my life I still had to play it out.

33

I was awakened by the sound of rain.

It was daylight. I went to the window. My room faced east. Lake Michigan, across the street, was kicking angrily at the breakwater. The rain, pushed by an erratic east wind, was striking the window in gusts.

I turned on the television set. The Channel 5 commentator was giving the local news in sign language for the deaf, speaking slowly as he went along, for the benefit of those who weren't deaf. He said nothing about Steve. The big story was still the impending teachers' strike. There'd also been a robbery at a supermarket; two policemen had been shot, one fatally.

I dressed. The bruise on my face was beginning to change color. It was going from black and blue to yellow and green. I needed a shave.

I called Burr. He wasn't in. I went down to breakfast, then tried twice again to reach Burr. He was in but busy.

Enough, I decided. I took a taxi to the Drake.

Olive and Livingston were having toast and coffee in their suite. Both looked tired. Neither appeared to be pleased by my visit. Especially after I said that I'd come to ask what was happening to Steve.

"I obtained a lawyer for him," Livingston admitted grudgingly.

"I know that," I said. "I saw him at the FBI office yesterday."

"There's nothing else I can tell you," Livingston said.

"Steve told them everything he knows," Olive put in.

Livingston shot her a look.

"Then why are they still holding him?" I asked.

No answer.

"When are they going to release him?" I asked.

"They want to show him some photographs," Livingston said after due consideration.

That I could understand. "Did they check his alibi?"

"Presumably," said Livingston.

I began to get angry. I tried not to show it. "I'm as anxious about this thing as you are," I reminded them.

"We've been asked not to reveal his whereabouts," Livingston said. "He's still in some danger."

Olive was doing her best to avoid looking at me but every now and then her eyes strayed briefly to my face. "I read something in the paper," she said finally, "about your having been shot the other day."

"Georgette's husband," I said.

"And you thought she was nice," she recalled acidly.

I almost gave up at that point. I hung in there, though. "You mentioned the hairdresser who used to own the shop she worked in," I said. "I located him Sunday afternoon. From him I got the address of his ex-wife. I went to see her. I was trying to find out if she knew where Steve was. There's evidently a relationship between her and Pepper Himes. After I left she went running to him. She must have told him I was on his trail, and he figured I was a threat. He's still looking for me, I believe."

"The sooner we all get out of this city, the better off we'll be," Olive said to Livingston.

A particularly strong gust of rain struck the window beside the table, as if to prove her point.

"Does that mean you intend to take Steve with you?" I asked.

"Naturally," said Livingston.

The doorbell sounded. Livingston and Olive exchanged glances. He got up to open the door.

Oscar Owen Nelson came into the room. Apparently they'd been expecting him.

"They're still waiting for some of the pictures to arrive from California," he said. Then he saw me. He didn't seem any happier with my presence than the others did.

"Where is Steve?" I asked.

"They're holding him," he replied tersely.

"Are they going to charge him with any crime?" I asked.

"I doubt it."

"Have they made any progress toward finding Himes?"

"You'll have to ask them that."

I doubled my effort to control my temper. "How much was he able to tell them?"

He wasn't exactly rude but he did make it evident that he wished I'd quit bothering him with questions and let him get down to business with the man he was going to send his bill to. I leaned back in my chair to indicate that I didn't intend to leave.

"It's the matter of protective custody," Nelson said to Livingston. "Steve has to agree to it."

"What do you recommend?" Livingston asked.

"There are two sides," Nelson said. "In protective custody he'd be less comfortable but safer. On the other hand, it might go on and on. For months."

"Where would they put him?" Olive asked. "Or would we

184

have bodyguards around the house all the time? What does it mean?"

"It can mean almost anything. In the case of a trial that's being prosecuted by the State's Attorney's office here, when they want to protect a witness who's going to testify for the prosecution, they put him in the witness quarters over in the Criminal Court Building. But this isn't in the hands of the State's Attorney yet. This is merely an investigation that's being conducted by the FBI on the one hand and a search for a murderer that's being conducted by the Police Department on the other. So far they haven't even caught anyone that they could bring to trial. So it could be a very long business." He paused. "You certainly wouldn't have bodyguards around all the time, though. The FBI doesn't train its men to be used that way and it can't afford to waste them."

"Well, then?" Olive asked.

"In some cases what they do is hide the person in a different city, to make it possible for him to get a job and a place to live under a different name until the time of the trial. And sometimes they use military installations. I think that's what they have in mind for Steve."

"Military installations?" Livingston asked.

"They use the stockade at Great Lakes Naval Training Station or at Fort Sheridan."

"You mean they'd keep Steve in prison?" Olive said.

"A military prison. It would be the safest place."

"Like a common criminal? I wouldn't consider anything like that!"

"Definitely not," Livingston agreed.

"Well," Nelson said as deferentially as he could, "it isn't altogether up to you. Steve is of age. He has to make his own decision. And to *agree* to be put in protective custody. I didn't get the feeling that that was what he wanted."

"He has to be protected," I said. "Pepper Himes is a desperate man. I know. He tried to kill me Sunday."

The three of them looked at me. Their expressions said, Who asked you?

"I don't know what Steve told the FBI about Pepper's accomplices but I do know that he saw Pepper try to kill Georgette in California—and so does Pepper. Something has to be done to keep him safe, at least as long as Pepper's at large."

"Precisely what is your interest in this matter, Mr. Jackson?" Nelson asked.

"I'd like to see Steve stay alive," I said. "I'm his father."

Livingston drew himself up to his full silvery height and said, "I beg to differ with you."

"Oh, hell," I said, and got up.

None of them made the slightest attempt to detain me as I went to the door.

Despite the rain, I walked around the block. And the block that the Drake Hotel sits on is like three regular blocks. By the time I got back to where I'd started from I was soaked. But no less angry.

I took a taxi to the FBI office.

Burr explained that he was very busy and could only see me for a few minutes.

He was sympathetic but firm. He told me that Steve wasn't there. He refused to tell me where Steve was. He did say that Steve had cooperated fully and that his alibi for the time of the murder was sound; he'd eventually be released. He was still being held, however, in the hope that he'd be able to identify as friends of Georgette certain people whose pictures were on file in California.

"What happens when he is released, Ed?" I asked.

"We're not sure yet," he replied.

"He has to be protected. Pepper hasn't given up. He went to my apartment again." I gave him the story Mrs. Moriarity had given me.

He grew thoughtful. "You were going to stay away from there."

"I did for one night. Then last night—well, I ended up staying away last night too. I went to the Holiday Inn on the Outer Drive."

"Continue to stay there."

I looked at him. "Just tell me one thing, Ed. How close do you think you are to catching Pepper?"

I wasn't sure what kind of an answer I'd get. I half expected an evasive one. But Burr was straightforward. "Walter, we've checked between a hundred and fifty and two hundred motels and hotels. He isn't at any of them, or if he is we don't know it. We're still checking—there are more men on this case, actually, than there ought to be—but frankly I'm disappointed. I suspect that he's staying with a friend—someone that we know nothing about. That's one of the reasons I want Steve to look at the photographs. If he can identify even one person, we'd have a lead. That person may have contacts in Chicago. As it is, we're working completely in the dark. Except for Mrs. Wayne—"

"And I spoiled that for you."

"Yes. Don't feel too badly, though. All of us do dumb things. I just realized that I did one too. I should have had a man stationed in your apartment. That was a blunder. But I didn't really believe that after having tried to kill you Himes would go there again. I didn't think it was a good idea for you to stay around there but I didn't seriously think—" His voice trailed off.

"Ed, do me one favor," I said. "Keep me posted on what's happening. I can't find out anything from Livingston, and if you don't tell me—"

"I'll try. It's tough, Walter. There's so much to do."

"It drives me nuts to keep calling here and not being able to talk to you."

"I know." He put his arm on my shoulder. "You're soaked, for Christ sake. Do you want to catch cold? Go back to the hotel. I'll be in touch with you. I have to go back to work now. I'm having a communications problem myself. I'm trying to get in touch with Carstairs, and he's out."

I did feel chilled. I walked across Jackson Boulevard to a

coffee shop and had two cups of hot coffee. I sat at the counter for almost a half-hour, warming up and thinking about what Burr had told me. Then I got a fistful of change and went to a public telephone.

Jack Kinney had moved but he was still in Las Vegas. He hadn't forgotten me any more than I'd forgotten him.

He wouldn't discuss anything with me on the telephone. If I'd come to Las Vegas, though, he said, he'd be glad to see me.

I drew money out of the bank and bought a plane ticket.

34

The young man who sat next to me reminded me of Terry Avalon. He was in his early twenties and was wearing a two-tone suede jacket, the tones being orange and dark brown. He was also wearing a ring. Not a diamond ring like Terry's but a star sapphire. The only difference between this young man and Terry was that when this one moved his arm I could see the cuff of his shirt, and it was frayed. Terry would never have worn a shirt with a frayed cuff.

He went to Las Vegas every three months, the young man told me. He also went to Puerto Rico occasionally. He liked Las Vegas better. More action. His game was craps. That was the only game that was worthwhile. He had his particular table at his particular hotel and he played his particular system. He was generous enough to explain the system to me, but I couldn't follow his explanation. When I tried to find out what he did besides go to Las Vegas and Puerto Rico he became so indefinite that I gathered he didn't do much of anything. I noticed that when he was talking about gambling he jiggled his knee in a way that reminded me of an automobile idling in neutral.

He was one of the first to get off the plane after it landed.

I found a taxi and gave the driver Jack's address, which was on Rancho Drive.

The house was a nice one, as were all of the houses around it, and looked as if it belonged on Rancho Drive. It was a ranch house. Most of the lights were on.

Jack opened the door himself and appeared surprised. "So soon?" he said.

"I'd have been here hours ago," I said, "but I couldn't get on any of the earlier flights."

He grinned. "Well, well, well. Well, well, well. You haven't changed a bit."

He himself had changed considerably. He'd been a thin, intense man who always concentrated utterly on the person he was speaking to, so that whatever he said seemed urgent. Now he was stout and relaxed and almost entirely bald.

"Well, don't just stand there," he said, taking my arm. "Come on in."

I went into the house. He led me across a large living room that had a copper hood over the fireplace and a leather-covered L-shaped sofa that must have taken the hides of a whole herd of cattle. We entered a sun room. This was evidently where Jack had been sitting. There was a half-consumed highball on a glass-topped end table and an open copy of *Sports Illustrated* beside it.

"Make yourself at home," Jack said. "Make yourself at home." He threw a wall switch, and the backyard was suddenly flooded with light. There was a cactus garden at one side and a kidney-shaped swimming pool in the middle.

"Not bad," I said. "Not bad at all."

"Picked the place up cheap ten years ago," he said. "Fellow who owned it went broke." He kept looking at me as if he couldn't believe I was actually there and he kept smiling. "Well, well, well. This takes me back a few years. It sure takes me back a few years. I never thought we'd meet up again. I sure didn't. Sit down. Let me fix you a drink. Just name it. I have everything anybody could want."

"Scotch," I said.

He tapped the wall, and a concealed door opened. There was a bar behind it. Very well stocked. Jack poured my drink. I took it over to a chair and sat down.

"Sorry I couldn't talk to you on the phone," Jack said, "but you know how it is."

I nodded. God, how he's changed, I thought. The change disturbed me. The Jack Kinney I'd known had been an up-and-coming hood who'd helped me ruin my life. But that Jack Kinney, I felt, was a man whom under certain circumstances I could trust. This Jack Kinney I knew nothing about. "How's the world been treating you?" I asked.

He seated himself heavily in a deep chair with yellow leather upholstery. "Not too bad, Walter. Not too bad. I'm retired now, you know. Retired a few years ago, after the wife died. The Feds don't seem to believe it. Every now and then they send people around to check up on me, but that's the way they are. They get something in their heads and they never get it out. But they never find anything."

They'd never found anything in the past either. But it had been there. "What do you do with yourself, Jack?"

"Dabble in real estate a little. Go over to L.A. every now and then. The older boy—he's studying biology at UCLA. The younger one—Billy—he's at UCLA too. I'm kind of worried about him, though. I'm afraid he might turn into some kind of hippie. I keep telling him I didn't raise no kid of mine to be no hippie, but you know how it is these days—you can't tell them anything." He sighed.

"Do you keep up with any of your old friends?"

His smile faded. His eyes narrowed. "Not much."

"I need a favor, Jack. As I was trying to tell you on the phone—"

"Favors, favors. Everyone always needs favors. I'm retired now. I don't do nobody any favors no more. I mind my own business."

"For old times' sake, Jack. I wouldn't have come all the way out here if it hadn't been important. I'm dying." If I could count on anyone to keep a secret it was Jack Kinney. His brain was a warehouse filled with undisclosed secrets.

"We're all dying. Every day we die one more day."

"But I'm dying pretty soon. I have Hodgkin's Disease. I haven't much time left. And there are a few things I'd like to straighten out before I go."

His manner became less guarded. He seemed genuinely surprised. And genuinely sorry. "No kidding? Well, now, that's a shame. It really is. Are you telling me the truth?"

"Yes. I wish I weren't."

"Hodgkin's Disease. Is that some form of cancer or something? The wife—she died of cancer."

"Yes. It's a form of cancer. Cancer of the lymph glands."

"Well, now, that's a Goddamn shame. I feel bad about it. I really do. Is that why your face is all messed up?"

"No, that's from something else. That's what I came to talk to you about."

He said nothing. But he seemed willing to listen.

I told him the whole story. When I finished he sat in his chair for a while, lost in thought. I couldn't guess what he was thinking. I hadn't been able to in the past and I couldn't now. I hoped, however, that he was thinking about the time I could have got him into trouble but didn't.

"All right," he said at last. That was all he said. Then he hoisted himself out of the chair and left the sun room.

He was gone for perhaps fifteen minutes. When he returned he said, "I called a friend of mine in L.A. He'll call me back in the morning."

We sat up half the night, reminiscing. He liked football almost as much as Burr did, although not for the same reasons. I couldn't help thinking, as Jack and I talked, that if he and Burr had been in different lines of work they'd probably have got along with each other very well.

About three o'clock in the morning Jack escorted me to the guest room and told me he hoped I'd be comfortable. I said I hated to impose on his hospitality. I wasn't imposing, he assured me—he was glad to have company; it got pretty lonesome sometimes.

We had breakfast in the kitchen. Jack cooked it himself. He didn't have a regular maid, he explained; just a woman who came in twice a week to clean. He didn't like having anyone around the place more than was necessary. He'd learned to cook and make beds himself during his wife's illness and kind of liked doing it.

I'd heard the telephone ring about seven o'clock. I'd wondered whether it was his friend in Los Angeles who was calling.

It had been. For when we were on our second cups of coffee Jack said, "I got some information on your man."

I looked at him expectantly, but he didn't go on. A change seemed to come over him. Although he was in his own kitchen he glanced around uneasily as if there might be someone eavesdropping.

"Come on," he said. "Bring your coffee outside."

We went into the yard.

"Is your place bugged?" I asked.

He shook his head. "But I never take chances." He walked me over to the cactus garden. The years seemed to fall away as he narrowed the distance between his face and mine and gazed at me with an intensity that demanded total attention. "I heard of this Himes before, couple of times. What I heard I didn't like. Now I hear he ain't changed much." He lowered his voice even more. "Loner," he said. "Works both sides of the fence."

"Both sides of the fence?" I asked, lowering my voice to the level of his.

"Friend of the cops, friend of the mob. You can't trust no one like that, and they can't trust no one either."

"But he got thrown off the force."

"They couldn't pin nothing on him except a bribe rap. The case wasn't strong enough to take to the jury but it was strong enough to get him kicked out of the Department. If they'd worked on it, they could have dug up plenty more but they didn't. He had friends. He still has friends. I ain't saying who they are, 'cause I don't know who they are, and the guy I talked to he don't know who they are—except one. Name of Danner. Detective. Follow him long enough and you might find the rest."

"But how can a man who got kicked off the force for taking a bribe—?"

"Because he's useful. The cops are always looking for information, and a guy like Pepper he's in a position he can give it to them. He's just got to be careful he doesn't give them too much or the wrong kind."

"But the men he's tied up with, who are pulling the robberies—"

"Shut up and listen. They need favors, the same as everyone else needs favors, the same as you come to me for a favor. If it weren't for favors everything would blow up and nobody would be anyplace. Pepper he was in a position he could get favors. Like you were telling me, when this Dave made that statement, Pepper found out about it right away, which makes him useful to the whole ring. And when there's money has to go back and forth, like it sometimes does, he's the one who can handle it. Understand?"

"I'm beginning to. There's no chance, then, that his buddies would try to kill him."

"Listen, Walter. That's what I just got through telling you. Sure there is. He has to be careful what he says and how much. They don't know he's giving the cops information. They just know he's got friends inside the Department and that he can get favors. Even if they think he might be stooling they don't think he's stooling on them—and he probably isn't. But if he does, and if they find out about it, then he can't figure on living very long. And if anyone in the law lets it out what he's been saying, as it sometimes happens, then there's hardly anyplace in the world he can go that's far enough."

"But if this friend of yours could get the information—"

"This friend of mine ain't just anybody, see. You asked me to do you a favor, and I did it. Not many people could have got that kind of favor from this particular guy."

"I see. Does this friend of yours say that that's what happened? That Pepper informed on his own friends?"

"I didn't ask him. Even he probably wouldn't know a thing like that. Sounds to me, though, from what you said, that somebody might have tipped the cops off about that job where the two guys got caught. If that's what happened, then Pepper's in a bad spot. But even if he didn't, if there's anybody who said that he did—like, say, this Georgette you were telling me about—"

"You think that's what happened?"

"How should I know? I think it's possible she may have threatened to."

"But why?"

"Why? Why does anybody do anything? Two reasons only. Love and money. This Georgette had both. She was in love with your son and she needed money."

I recalled Burr's suspicion of blackmail. He hadn't been so wrong. "Then Pepper must think that Georgette told Steve and Steve told me."

"Looks that way. She must have known the risk she was taking and tried to protect herself like people do. 'If you kill me, my friend will tell everything he knows.' "

"Besides which, Steve saw him actually try to kill her."

Jack moved away from me. The dangerous information had already been given. "There's that too. And he might figure that Steve told you, since you went asking Mrs. Wayne about him."

"And I could testify that he tried to kill me."

Jack nodded. Then he frowned. Not at me—at one of the cactus plants. It had a broken branch. "It wasn't like that yesterday," he said. "Keeping up a place is a lot of damn work," he added with a sigh.

I wondered whether the cactus garden had come with the house or whether Jack had cultivated it himself. What was the fascination of plants that dared you to touch them? "Of the two reasons," I said, "I think that money was more important than love. I saw Georgette and Steve together. She was already beginning to get bored with him, I think. Just as he was with her."

"You never know about things like that," Jack said. "Sometimes a tough broad can be an awful sucker for a guy who isn't as tough as she is. Just like a smart broad can be an awful sucker for a dumb guy. Some of them kind of like to protect. I seen plenty."

"The other thing I wanted to know—"

Jack drew close to me again. I could actually feel his breath on my face as he said, "Pepper Himes has got no friends that I could find out about in Chicago. Danner knows somebody, though. Once was a cop too, now's a private dick. Name's Kohler—Archie Kohler. Been in Chicago maybe five, six years."

"Thank you, Jack. Thank you very much."

He backed away and suddenly he grinned. "Let's go into the house. It's time for you to do me a favor."

The favor he wanted was for me to give him my opinion on the next weekend's football games.

We spent an hour going over the card. Then he called his bookie. He bet on half a dozen games. A total of twelve thousand dollars.

He insisted on driving me to the airport. When we shook hands I had a strange feeling. It was as if a chapter of my life which I'd thought would never really end had finally ended. Jack must have felt something too, for he hung on to my hand longer than was necessary.

"I don't suppose we'll ever meet again," he said.

"It's not likely," I said. Then I opened the door of the car and got out.

196

35

It was no longer raining in Chicago, but the temperature had dropped considerably, and the streets were slippery. It took the taxi driver almost an hour to get me from the airport to the Holiday Inn.

I bought a newspaper in the shop off the lobby and worked my way through the crowd of conventioneers who were checking in at the desk. There were some messages in my box. The room clerk gave them to me along with my key.

Mr. Burr had called at one-thirty and wanted me to call him back. Mr. Burr had called at three-fifteen and wanted me to call him back. Mr. Burr had called at four-ten and wanted me to call him back.

I went up to my room and dialed FBI headquarters. Mr. Burr had gone for the day. I explained to the operator that he'd been trying to reach me and asked her to relay the information that I was now at the hotel.

I looked through the newspaper. There was nothing in it about Pepper's having been picked up. But presently I saw an item which undoubtedly explained why Burr had been trying to get in touch with me. Steve had been released.

The article was short and was hidden away in the inside corner of the page opposite the obituaries. Innocence was less newsworthy than guilt, apparently. But the fact that the story was in the newspaper at all made me uneasy.

I found the telephone directories in a drawer. There was no listing for an Archie Kohler in the alphabetical directory or in the yellow pages. It was possible that he worked for one of the large agencies, I thought, and that his private number was unlisted. Or else he lived in the suburbs. There were no suburban directories in the room.

After half an hour Burr called.

"Where the hell have you been?" he wanted to know.

"Out of town," I said.

"I needed you."

"I saw in the paper that Steve was released."

"That's why I was calling. He wouldn't go along with any sort of protective custody, and the lawyer that Livingston hired—"

"Where did Steve go?"

"Back to Livingston's. Maybe you can still talk to him."

"I don't know what I'd say."

"Tell him he's a damn fool."

"Evidently you haven't found Pepper yet."

"No."

"I think that you and I'd better get together for a few minutes, Ed. I got some information while I was away that may help you. It's about Pepper."

"I'll come down to the hotel. Meanwhile talk to your son."

"If he's with Livingston they may not even let me through to him. I'll try, though."

We hung up, and I called the Drake.

The Livingstons, I was told, had checked out.

It was after nine o'clock when Burr arrived. He looked weary. The day hadn't been a good one, he admitted. Steve hadn't been able to identify even one of the pictures he'd been shown. As far as Burr was concerned, no progress whatsoever had been made toward breaking up the ring of jewel thieves. If anything, the investigation had lost ground since the first time he'd talked to me. Then at least there'd been the possibility of learning something from Georgette.

I told him that the Livingstons had left the hotel. He swore. But then he said, "I don't suppose we could expect them to stay around here, though. They got their son back. That's what they really came for. Personally I think he was foolish not to let us look after him."

I nodded. Yet it seemed to me that in Steve's place I might have made the same decision. To be locked up in a military prison for months, even if it were for my own good, wouldn't have appealed to me. "Can you protect him from a distance?" I asked.

"How can you protect anyone from a distance? We'll keep tabs on him. I made that pretty damn clear. But you can't protect anyone who's free to go wherever they please. It just isn't possible."

"I wish I could have done something. I don't like the idea of his going back to California. Aside from the danger, even. I'd hoped—" I stopped. What had I hoped? That somehow I could recover all the lost years? Impossible. "But let me tell you what I found out."

I gave him all the information Jack had given me about Pepper's double role as informer to the police and to his criminal friends. He wanted to know where I'd got my facts. From a retired hood who owed me a favor, I said. I was prepared to resist if he pressed me for Jack's name, but he didn't. He didn't seem particularly surprised by what I had to say, but when I gave him Danner's name he suddenly got interested. He immediately placed a call to the FBI office, in Los Angeles.

"That opens up a whole new avenue," he told me.

"Then there's something else you can work on," I said. "Danner has a friend here in Chicago. Also a former policeman. His name's Archie Kohler. He's supposed to be working as a private detective."

Burr placed a second call. To someone named Webb at the Chicago office of the FBI. He told him to get to work on Kohler at once.

The weariness seemed to have disappeared. He looked happy. "Maybe we should have arrested you instead of your son," he said. "You're the one who had the information."

"If it weren't for your arresting him I wouldn't have got it. How much does it really help you, though?"

"That depends. In this business you learn not to expect miracles. These investigations go on for months, sometimes years. We've been working on this one for a long time already—that's how we came across your son in the first place. Now, with the information you've given us, maybe we'll make some headway. It isn't going to happen right away—it wouldn't have anyhow. I wish I could say that every case we work on leads to a mass arrest of the whole gang, but it doesn't often happen that way. If it did, organized crime in this country would have ended years ago."

"I suppose you're right. But I hope that at least you get Pepper pretty soon."

"So do I. And if this Kohler knows anything, maybe we will. But getting Pepper isn't the answer to everything. He's only one cog in the wheel, after all. And he might not talk. His kind often doesn't."

"He's a killer, though. He murdered his wife. And at the moment I believe he intends to murder Steve."

"We certainly aren't going to give up on him. But the one who interests me even more is this Danner."

Our interests were beginning to diverge, it appeared. Burr was thinking about the future. I, on the other hand, was still concerned about the present.

He seemed to sense what was going through my mind. "Personally I don't have much use for Livingston," he said, "but I do believe that he's aware of the danger Steve is in and that he'll

200

try to keep him safe. And if money is what it takes, then there's really nothing for you to worry about." He paused, then added, "Except yourself. You're on Pepper's list too."

"Does he know that Steve's on his way to California?"

"It's pretty hard to know what he knows and what he doesn't. He seems to be pretty good at finding things out. And if Kohler's helping him—"

"It was in the evening paper that Steve was released."

"I know. I'm sorry. I didn't give out the information, but somebody did."

"So we can assume that if Pepper doesn't know right this minute that Steve's on his way to California, it won't be long before he does. That's why I'm worried. Steve is more of a threat to him, I think he thinks, than I am. And since he can't be in two places at once he'll go after Steve first. So for the moment I don't think I'm in much danger."

"You never know." He frowned. "I did have a man over at your place yesterday and the day before. He didn't find anyone trying to get in or loitering around. Nevertheless—"

"My next-door neighbor saw him leaving, like I told you, so he may not want to take any more chances."

"What are your plans, though?"

"I'll probably go away," I said. And suddenly everything crystallized. "In fact, I'm definitely going away. To Jamaica."

"Jamaica? That's something new, isn't it? For how long?"

"Until the end."

He regarded me somberly. "You ought to have somebody with you."

I shook my head.

"When will you leave?"

"As soon as I get things wound up here. It shouldn't take more than a week."

"I'll keep in touch with you. If you're smart you'll stay right here at the hotel until you leave."

"That wouldn't do much good. I'm going to have to go to my office, and there are things at my apartment which I need. No,

I'm going to go on with my life as usual and hope for the best. If and when you catch Pepper you'll have Steve as a witness against him, and I—well, we've been through that already."

Burr said nothing. He sat there for a while, staring at the rug, then got up. "You know what's best for you, I guess. I'd kind of hoped you'd be around for a while, but maybe you're doing the right thing. We'll see each other before you go."

"Keep an eye on Steve."

He nodded. We shook hands. He thanked me for the information I'd given him. I went with him to the door.

"I won't say good-bye," he said with a tight smile. "I'll see you in a day or two."

"Sure," I said. But it seemed to me that this was a good-bye of sorts. Steve had been the cause of our coming together, and Steve—at least as far as I was concerned—was no longer in the picture. "Thanks again for the book."

"The book? Oh. Well, it isn't every case that gives me a chance to meet one of my early heroes."

I smiled. Even though it hurt my face to do so.

36

After breakfast I checked out of the hotel and drove home. I shaved and took a hot shower and changed the dressing on my thigh. Then I spent a few minutes thinking about the things that had to be done.

The furniture, the clothes—they could stay where they were. The executor of my estate would eventually dispose of them.

The daily newspaper, the bills that were coming due, the appointments that Fenwick had wanted me to make for periodic checkups, the wedding of Dick Norwood's daughter which I was supposed to attend, the clothes that were at the laundry —the little things, the minor details that gave continuity to life, could be disposed of or ignored. Most of them, I decided, I'd ignore.

But there were a couple of major things that I couldn't ignore. I had to make a will and I had to set things up with Charly. I called my lawyer and made an appointment with him for eleven o'clock. Then I called Charly and invited him to have lunch with me.

The biggest item of all I did nothing about. That was Rita. I tried to force myself to think about her, to decide what I was going to say, but my mind kept turning away from the issue. Perhaps later, it promised, after the will was signed, after the arrangements with Charly were made, it would present me with an answer.

I left my apartment at ten and drove downtown. After parking I still had three quarters of an hour to kill before going to the lawyer's. I passed the time shopping for a wedding gift for Dick Norwood's daughter. I selected a silver bread tray and sent it, then strolled slowly across the Loop to La Salle Street. I was amazed at how good I suddenly felt. No responsibilities, no problems—how many people were there in the world who ever found themselves in a position where they could say to hell with everything and simply walk away?

Riding up to my lawyer's floor in the elevator, I again thought of Rita—but only for an instant; my mind still refused to function in that area. And I wondered briefly about Steve and Burr. Was Steve back in the enormous house in Bel-Air? Had Burr managed to locate Archie Kohler? There was no point in dwelling on those questions either, though. I'd done what I could. What happened from now on was beyond my control.

"I want to make a will," I told the lawyer, "and I want to sign it right here and now."

He objected. It would have to be typed. That would take time.

"I'll make it very simple," I said. "I want to leave everything outright to a Mrs. Rita Swift and I want you to act as executor." I had a fleeting thought about Steve but I dismissed it. Even if he inherited only a part of what Livingston had and a part of what Olive's father would leave he'd still be one of the richest men in the United States.

By the time everything was properly worded it was almost noon. I'd told Charly to meet me at King Arthur's Pub at twelve-fifteen. The lawyer said that even if the stenographer delayed her lunch the document wouldn't be ready for signature until one. I agreed to come back.

"Why after all these years the sudden rush?" he wanted to know.

"I'm going on a trip," I told him.

He seemed satisfied with that answer.

Charly was already at the restaurant when I arrived. I found him at a table with a drink in front of him. "You look better today," he greeted me. "You must have had a good night's sleep."

"I suddenly feel carefree," I replied. "Or at least I will when I get through with you."

The waiter came over. I pointed to Charly's drink and said, "Make it two." Then I turned to Charly. "Here's what I want you to do. Get up a letter for me to sign, to go out to all my clients, saying that I'm turning my business over to you. Then start going through my files. You ought to have a complete list of every policy that each client has—policy number, name of the company the policy is placed with, terms, everything. I think we ought to notify the companies also. Then have your lawyer draw up whatever papers you or he thinks are necessary. After that—"

"Wait a minute, wait a minute. This is all going to take time."

"That's the one thing we haven't got, Charly. Within a week I intend to be gone."

"But what about your son? You said you were going to get us together. You said—"

"I know. Well, he's gone back to California."

"I see. And Ben Small—"

"I'll go to your office with you from here. We'll try to talk to him. He's supposed to be in town today. I'll explain the situation, and we'll see what he says. If he isn't here, then you'll just have to talk to him on your own as soon as you can. Meanwhile . . ." I continued with the list of steps that I thought would be necessary for Charly to take within the next few days.

I accompanied him to his office after lunch and placed a call to Ben. He was in conference. I asked Nancy Morris whether he planned to spend the night in the house at Lake Forest. She said yes. I said to tell him I'd call him there later.

"I think I'll be able to reach him this evening," I said to Charly. "I'll let you know in the morning what he says." I glanced across the air shaft to my own office. It was dark. "Here are the keys to my place. Get started with the files as soon as you can." I remembered the letters at the public stenographer's. I told him to pick them up, that I'd be in later to sign them.

"Where are you going now?" he asked.

To sign my will, I almost said. "To see a man. Get started, Charly."

"But, Walter—"

"Don't cock around, pal. You'll find everything in good order. I may be a lousy insurance salesman but I'm a hell of a record-keeper."

I went back to the lawyer's and signed the will. His stenographer and his switchboard operator witnessed the signature.

I started for my office but on the way I thought of something else that needed doing. Although I'd wanted for years to go to Jamaica I really didn't know anything about the place. It was time to find out. I had a client who worked for a travel agency. I went to see her.

She showed me some folders. I picked a hotel. "When do you want to leave?" she asked.

I hesitated. How long would it take Charly to go through the files and get the necessary papers drawn up? "A week from tomorrow," I said.

She called the airline and the hotel representative and made the reservations for me.

"By the way," I said, "I may be turning my business over to another broker soon. I'm thinking of retiring. His name is Charlton Kipness. You'll get a formal letter telling you about it, but I just thought I'd mention it."

"Is that a fact?" she said. She didn't appear to care much one way or the other. I hoped the rest of the clients would react with as much indifference, for Charly's sake.

One more matter disposed of, I thought as I walked back to the office. Now the die was definitely cast. Jamaica.

Charly was sitting at my desk. The desk was covered with files.

"Your friend Rita called," he informed me as I was taking off my coat.

I stopped for a moment. "Oh?" Then I hung my coat on the clothes tree.

"She was kind of upset," Charly went on. "She's been trying to reach you since yesterday."

"I'm going to have to decide," I said, more to myself than to him.

"She's at her office," he said. "She wants you to call her there."

I nodded. "Did you pick up the letters at the stenographer's?"

"Yes. They're around here somewhere."

We looked for them. They were under a stack of files. I signed them.

"I guess your son changed his mind about going to California," Charly said.

I looked up. "What makes you say that?"

"Because," Charlie replied, "according to Rita, he's at her place."

37

So many feelings hit me at once that I couldn't separate them. Sorrow. Anxiety. Gratitude. And an absurd joy.

For a moment sorrow was dominant. His eyes showed an irretrievable loss of youth. The last vestiges of innocence were gone. But then happiness took over. He'd chosen to stay; the bond that I'd felt he'd felt too.

Even after I swallowed, my voice was hoarse. "What the hell?" I said.

His voice wasn't quite steady either. "I called your apartment last night, but nobody answered, so I called here."

"How did you get the number, son?"

"You gave it to me."

I thought back. So I had. It seemed like a very long time ago. "You didn't go to California with your mother?"

He shook his head.

"Do you realize the danger you're in here?"

He nodded. Then he said, "I couldn't go back there, Dad. Not after everything that's happened. It'd be like it was before, and—" He turned up his palms and shrugged.

It took a while to get the story from him, and when it did come it came in bits and pieces. Two FBI men had driven him to the Drake. Oscar Owen Nelson had accompanied them. Steve had been emotionally shaken by his arrest, by the two nights he'd spent in the hands of the law, by the interrogation he'd been put through and by the dispute with Burr over the matter of protective custody. His anger at Livingston hadn't yet spent itself, and he'd been dismayed to learn from Nelson that his mother also was in Chicago. It had been a bad climate for a reunion.

Livingston, I suspected, was genuinely concerned about Steve's safety. Olive too. But apparently neither of them had succeeded in getting that point across. Livingston had started by reproaching Steve for getting himself into such a mess and by listing the expenses he'd incurred on Steve's account. Olive had added fuel to the fire by accusing him of being ungrateful and of having disgraced her.

The upshot had been a short, violent quarrel which even Nelson couldn't mediate. And Steve had stormed out of the suite at the Drake much as he'd stormed out of Livingston's house a year before.

I felt obliged to say, "You should have let the FBI put you in a safe place while Pepper's still on the loose."

"In a jail? Two days was enough. I couldn't take any more of that, Dad. You don't know what it's like."

I didn't argue. I simply said, "I'm glad you're here."

And right after that Rita arrived. With her own set of conflicting emotions. She was angry that I hadn't called her since Tuesday, relieved that nothing drastic had happened to me, pleased to see Steve and me reunited and puzzled by something which she didn't mention at first but which turned out to be the fact that Charly had told her he was going through my files.

I didn't try to account for Charly's statement about the files. Instead I suggested drinks and while we were drinking I described my trip to Las Vegas.

Rita and Steve were amazed. Steve more than Rita. At first he refused to admit even the possibility that Georgette might have threatened to expose Pepper but then he grew thoughtful. "She wouldn't do it for money," he said.

I couldn't imagine her doing it for any other reason, but I said nothing.

"She wanted to get away from him," he said. "She wanted to get away from all of them. She wanted to be with me."

To an extent, I conceded silently, that may have been true. Although Steve had had no money when they met she certainly must have known that someday he'd be very rich. But in the meantime they had to eat, and Georgette had been a practical woman. "Well, anyway," I said, "she somehow managed to make Pepper feel threatened enough to want to kill her."

"And now me," Steve added.

"And now you," I agreed. "That's why the first thing we're going to do is let Mr. Burr know where you are."

"If he knows, then pretty soon Pepper will know," Steve objected.

"Now that the FBI is aware of the leak I'm sure they'll be careful," I said, and ended any further discussion by going to the telephone and calling the FBI office.

Burr had gone for the day, as I'd expected, but I left an urgent message for him to get in touch with me at Rita's number.

The three of us brightened after that. None of the basic problems had been solved, but with Burr about to enter the picture some of them at least seemed a little less serious. Rita began to work on the sleeping arrangements. They were complicated, she said, by the fact that Julie was going to be there too.

"Again?" I asked.

"Swell," Steve said.

"One of Terry's friends is getting married tomorrow," Rita explained, "and Julie's invited to the wedding. Terry's meeting her at the station."

I glanced at Steve and had a fleeting vision of him and Julie as a couple. It would be nice, I thought. Then I glanced at Rita, wondering whether she thought so too.

"Your father doesn't approve of my daughter's boyfriend," she told Steve.

"I approve of your daughter, though," I said.

Steve smiled a smile which for an instant made me feel that he was older than I was.

One thought about his future led to another, however, and when Rita went into the kitchen to get dinner started I called Ben Small.

He was at home and he was alone—his wife had remained in Palm Beach. He'd be glad to see me.

After I hung up I sat at the telephone, debating whether or not to take Steve to Lake Forest with me. It would be difficult to speak frankly with Ben in Steve's presence. On the other hand, it was important for the two of them to meet. I decided to take him.

Over dinner I broached the subject. "This may not be the time to bring it up," I said, "but I'm going to anyway." And I proceeded to outline my plan for Steve to go into the insurance business. I told him about Charly Kipness and said that it might be better for him to start with Charly than to start with me.

His expression was one of mild surprise and mild interest. "I hadn't got around to thinking that far ahead," he admitted.

"I don't suppose you have," I said, "but it's important that you do."

"You're going at this thing much too fast," Rita said, giving me a reproachful look. "It's going to take a while for things to sort themselves out."

I ignored her. "The man I owe more to than to anyone else is Ben Small. He's chairman of the board of Carling-Small Laboratories. He was a friend when I needed one and he's been a friend through the years. Even now the bulk of my business comes from him. I talked to him a little while ago, and he's in town just for tonight. Tomorrow he's leaving for Washington. I made a date to go out to see him. I'd like you to come along."

"Sure," Steve said.

"Walter!" Rita said sharply. "It's ridiculous for you to go out when that murderer may be—"

"Rita, please! That murderer doesn't even know that you exist, let alone that Steve or I are with you. And if I say that this is important then it's important."

Rita started to speak but checked herself. She'd learned over the years that Ben and I didn't get together often but that a meeting with him took precedence over everything else. "Suit yourself," she said more mildly. "All I mean is that Steve's career isn't the most important thing in the world right now. There's plenty of time to think about it."

"From Washington Ben is going to Tokyo," I said, "and there's no telling when he'll be in town again."

"I know one of the Carling kids," Steve put in. "We were in the same dorm one semester."

"That's helpful," I said.

The tension eased.

Rita frowned at the fried perch on her plate. "I don't know why I bought fish," she said. "I never did like it."

The telephone rang. I thought it might be Burr so I answered it myself.

It was Burr. "Whose number is this?" he wanted to know.

"Rita's," I said.

"Are you staying with her?"

"Yes. And Steve is with me."

"Steve?"

"That's why I wanted to talk to you. He didn't go to California. He decided to stay here with me."

"I think I'd better send a couple of men over to have a look around. What's the address?"

"I don't think it's necessary, Ed. No one knows we're here. No one except you."

"You're probably right, but I'd feel better if I did. We got a line on Kohler today."

"You did?"

"He's a private detective, all right. Or at least he was. The

212

reason he wasn't listed in the telephone directory is he was a house detective in a hotel and he lived there too."

"That explains it."

"I said was. They fired him a few months ago because of some jewel robberies in the place. Interesting, eh?"

"Very."

"The thing is, he didn't leave any forwarding address, and we don't know where to locate him now. I have a crazy idea that —well, you didn't by chance get the feeling that anybody was following you today, did you?"

"No."

"I suppose not. And you probably wouldn't know it if anybody was. But I'd feel better if I had a couple of men on hand, just in case."

"That's all right with me." I gave him Rita's address. As an afterthought I added that I was planning to take Steve out to Lake Forest with me after dinner.

"Don't leave until my men get there," Burr said. "Please. I can have them there within an hour."

I agreed, and we hung up.

Rita was pleased when I told her of the arrangements. Steve seemed to think it was a good idea too.

"As long as we're going to have some protection," I said to Rita, "Steve and I'll spend the night at my place. That'll give you room for Julie."

Rita agreed that it might be better that way. "Let's hope they catch that man Pepper soon," she added. "Then we can go back to leading normal lives again."

"They're getting closer," I said. "They're trying to trace Archie Kohler and they've made some progress." About going back to a normal life, however, I said nothing.

38

The FBI men arrived within forty-five minutes. Their names were Hill and Timmons. They'd circled the block and checked the building before coming inside, they said; there were no loiterers.

"Did Mr. Burr explain to you that my son and I are going to Lake Forest?" I asked.

"Yes," Timmons replied. "Our instructions are to go with you."

I didn't like the idea of arriving at Ben's with an escort, but as it turned out the problem didn't arise. Hill and I drove my car back to the garage in my building while Timmons and Steve followed us in the FBI car. Then Hill and I got in with them, and the four of us drove to Lake Forest without incident. When we pulled up under the porte-cochere of the sprawling Tudor mansion that Ben's father had built fifty years ago, the FBI men themselves suggested that they wait outside.

The other problem I'd anticipated—that of arranging to speak to Ben in private—took care of itself also. After a few minutes of getting acquainted with Steve and showing him the billiard room, which had always been a particular source of pride to Ben, he said to me, "I wonder if I can see you alone," and led me into the library.

"I had a peculiar telephone call just before leaving the office this evening," he began. "From a Mr. Charlton Kipness, who said that you're retiring and that he's taking over your business. Why are you smiling?"

"Good old Charly," I said. "He's suddenly got more ambition than he knows what to do with. But it's true, Ben. That's what I wanted to talk to you about."

"But, Walter, you're too young."

I hadn't known until that moment what I was going to say, but suddenly all doubt left me. "There's more to it than that, Ben. I'm not retiring. I'm dying. I have Hodgkin's Disease."

Ben looked so stricken that for an instant I was sorry I'd told him.

"I had to tell you, Ben. You've been a good friend to me over the years and you're entitled to know. But as of right now I haven't told Steve and I'd appreciate your not saying anything." I went on to outline what I had in mind as far as my insurance clients were concerned and then to explain about Steve. As briefly as I could I described his break with Livingston and his recent difficulties. "I'm worried about him," I concluded. "Not as much as I was a few days ago—he's matured a great deal in a very short period of time—but he's too young to make it without some sort of guidance and without some of the help that I might have been able to give him if things were different."

"Of course," Ben said. "Don't worry about a thing. If it were up to me, I'd place him with one of the big firms, though. An outfit like Anderson, Atkins, Allen and Smith—they handle quite a bit of business for the company. Then when he's learned the ropes I'll make him my personal insurance man. Let this Kipness handle your other clients. I'll see that Steve is looked after."

"That would be the greatest favor you could do me, Ben."

"I've been wanting to consolidate all of our insurance business anyway. But this other news—I mean, about yourself—that's a blow, Walter. I can't tell you how much of a blow. If only there were some way—"

"There isn't, Ben. There's a certain date for all of us, and mine is coming up. It's going to be easier, though, now that I know Steve'll be all right."

Ben nodded slowly. "Maybe we'd better have a drink," he said. "I kind of feel the need of one."

We had the drink, then I invited Steve to join us. He and Ben spent a few more minutes getting acquainted, and they seemed to take to each other.

"You resemble your father quite a bit," Ben told him.

"I'm afraid I'll never be a football player," Steve said.

"But you might make a pretty good insurance man," Ben said.

Steve grinned.

And not long after that we left.

Hill and Timmons escorted us up to my apartment and searched the place. They found nothing suspicious. They also checked the corridor and the fire stairs. Nothing there either.

"What happens now?" I asked.

"That's up to you," Hill said. "If you stay in your apartment you'll be all right. If you go out—at least for the time being—you should have somebody with you. Do you think it would be possible for you to stay inside for a few days?"

I turned to Steve. "I can if you can," I said.

"It's all right with me," he said.

"At least over the weekend," Timmons said. "By then, let's hope, everything will be cleared up."

"Let's hope," I agreed.

"If for any reason you should want to go out, though, please contact the office. We'll send somebody over."

"Tell Burr where we are," I said. "And to let me know in case anything happens."

They said that they would and left.

"Looks like I ended up in protective custody after all," Steve said with a smile.

"I think it's rather a good idea," I said.

"I don't mind. Not as long as it's like this. I'm really kind of glad. There are an awful lot of things I'd like to ask you."

"Such as?"

"What you were doing all the time I was growing up."

"That'll take quite a while. I'd better make some coffee."

I made the coffee, but we didn't talk about the things I'd done while he was growing up. It seemed to me that it was more important for us to talk about his future, and I led the conversation around to that. I told him what Ben had suggested in the way of a job for him.

"But I don't know anything about the insurance business," he said.

"You'll learn," I assured him.

"What about you, though? After I learn, would I come in with you?"

I was tempted to answer him truthfully but instead I evaded the issue. "We'll see. But in the meanwhile if you should ever need any help and I shouldn't be around I hope you'll go to Ben. He's been a great friend to me, and I'm sure he'll be one to you too." Then I changed the subject altogether. "What's your honest opinion of Julie Swift?" I asked.

"I just met her for a minute," he replied. "She seems swell."

"I hope that in time you'll get to know her better," I said.

Steve gave me another of those smiles which made me feel that of the two of us I was the less mature. "You seem to have done a lot of thinking about what I'm going to do," he said. "What about what you're going to do?"

"Well, the first thing I'm going to do," I said, "is cancel some reservations I have to go to Jamaica. After I get some sleep, that is. I hope you don't mind if I take the bedroom this time."

He eyed the couch critically. "How will I fit on that thing?"

"The same way I did," I replied. "Fold yourself up."

He tried it. He found that it worked. He was asleep long before I was.

I tossed and turned for an hour. I finally came to the conclusion that I was going to level with Steve and with Rita just as I'd leveled with Ben, and shortly after that I dozed off.

Eventually I must have fallen into a very deep sleep, however, for when the telephone woke me I felt completely disoriented.

"Mr. Jackson?" a man said.

"Yes," I replied, trying to find the light switch.

"Captain Edwards, Eighteenth District police headquarters. Is your son with you? Steven Livingston?"

"Yes. What's the matter?"

"We've just arrested a man we believe to be Francis Himes. We'd like you to bring your son over here to identify him in a lineup."

The web of sleep disintegrated. I sat bolt upright. "You did? When? We'll be right over."

"I'll send two men to pick you up. Can you be outside, in front of your building, in fifteen minutes?"

"Sure. In even less than that."

"Fifteen minutes. They'll be there. Thank you." He hung up.

I went into the living room. Steve had slept through the ringing of the telephone. I shook him.

He sat up. "What's the matter?"

"They've caught Pepper. They want us to come over to identify him."

He rubbed his eyes. "Both of us?"

"Yes. They're going to pick us up in fifteen minutes."

"Can't it wait?" he asked. Then he too came fully awake. "They did? They caught Pepper?"

"Right. They want us to pick him out of a police lineup."

He swung his legs off the couch. "This is going to give me one

218

hell of a lot of pleasure," he said, reaching for his pants.

"No more than it's going to give me," I said, and went into the bedroom to dress.

We were downstairs in less than ten minutes. We were waiting at the curb when the car approached.

I didn't recognize the man who was behind the wheel but I recognized the man who was sitting next to him. It was Pepper Himes. And he was pointing a gun through the open window.

39

Steve reacted faster than I. I heard him yell, "Look out!" and felt the impact of his body at the same moment.

I landed on the sidewalk on my right side but recovered immediately and scrambled toward the shelter of a parked car. Steve had thrown himself down directly behind me but was rolling in the opposite direction, across the clearing made by the two NO PARKING signs in front of the building.

Pepper fired once through the open window of the car. I heard the soft pop of the gun and the ping of the bullet as it struck the pavement.

Steve kept rolling and reached the protection of the car next to the sign at the far side of the entrance.

"Help!" I shouted at the top of my voice.

Pepper opened the door and jumped to the street.

"Help!" I shouted again.

Steve ducked into the space between the first car and the second at the instant that Pepper's foot touched the sidewalk. Pepper looked both ways and saw me. I sprang as he turned to fire. Without the sore leg I might have connected with him but as it was I fell short.

"Eeeah!" Steve hollered, coming out from between the two cars.

I saw Pepper's foot move as he turned to fire at Steve. I stretched and caught his ankle with both hands. I pulled.

The gun popped again, but the bullet missed. Steve ducked back between the cars.

Pepper's foot moved the other way. I yanked his ankle. He fired and lost his balance simultaneously. I felt a sting on my right side below the rib cage. As if the flame of a match had touched me. Pepper staggered. The gun popped a fourth time. A fragment of concrete struck my face. I opened my mouth to utter another shout, but just then everything turned black and I was aware only of weight as first Pepper and then Steve fell on top of me.

The weight shifted as they struggled. I tried to get out from under. I heard grunts and hissing, then I heard a window open.

"Stop that racket!" a woman cried.

"Help!" I called, but the sound was muffled by the bodies on top of me.

A car door opened. Shoes scraped on the street.

"I'll call the police!" the woman cried. "Police!"

Another window opened. A man's voice yelled, "What's going on out there?"

"Call the police!" the woman replied to him.

Brakes squealed as a passing car stopped.

I made another effort to get the pitching weight off my back but I couldn't do it.

"Hey, you guys!" a man called from the street.

"Call the police!" the woman at the window screamed.

Another car door opened. A woman cried in a panicky voice, "Come back here, Henry, you'll get hurt!"

A different gun fired. It made more noise. The woman in the car shrieked.

Pepper's gun popped. Someone went, "Ahhh." It was a long,

slow sound and it came from right behind my ear.

The woman in the car continued to shriek.

"Police!" screamed the woman at the window. "Police! A man's been shot! Police!"

Half of the weight slid off my back. I rolled out from under the other half. Steve was lying on the sidewalk, Pepper was scrambling to his feet. He still had the gun but he wasn't aiming it. I threw myself against his legs. He went down on one knee. I tried to butt him with my head but only grazed his thigh. He shifted the gun. I swung my hand. The gun flew into the air.

The woman in the car kept up her shrieking.

I heard the gun land but didn't see it. My right side was beginning to go numb. Pepper got up. I tried to get up also but only made it to my knees. Pepper looked toward the street. "Archie!" he called, and started toward the car. He didn't get to it in time, though, for Archie was once more behind the wheel, and as Pepper reached the handle of the open door the car sped off. The backspin of the door sent him reeling against the fender of one of the parked cars.

A man lay on the pavement. He was motionless. His car was double-parked on the other side of the street, one door open. The woman inside the car was still shrieking hysterically.

I glanced at Steve. He too was motionless. I crawled to him. In the glow of the streetlight I could see blood streaming from a wound in his right shoulder. It seemed to be coming from front and back at the same time. A pool was forming under his right arm. "Help!" I shouted.

Pepper turned. He came toward me.

I heard a siren in the distance. Be a police car, I prayed. And come this way.

Another car approached. It pulled up in back of the car with the screaming woman.

Pepper spotted the gun and went for it.

Two men jumped out of the car that had just pulled up. They saw the man lying in the street and stopped. They stood there transfixed.

Still on my hands and knees, I tried to get between Pepper and the gun. I felt a blinding pain in my side as the toe of his shoe connected with my shoulder. And I felt the gun under me as I fell.

The siren grew louder.

Pepper's foot went back to kick again. I made an effort to block it with my arm. I didn't succeed entirely but I deflected it toward my shoulder.

The two men in the street started toward us.

I braced myself for a third blow, but it didn't come. Pepper hesitated a moment, then began to run. I wanted to get the gun out from under me and fire it at him but I was too weak. I simply lay there on it while the woman in the car continued to pierce the air with her screams and the siren came closer.

The men reached me. "Are you all right?" one of them asked.

All I was able to say was, "Call the FBI."

And a moment later the siren sped past. It wasn't attached to a police car. It was attached to an ambulance.

40

Kohler was arrested within the hour. For speeding through a stop sign and attempting to shoot the arresting officer.

Kohler supplied the information that Pepper Himes had been living in a hotel room which Sally Wayne had rented under her maiden name. Pepper was captured there later that morning. He was injured when he attempted to break through the police trap, but his injury wasn't serious.

The motorist who'd stopped to help was named Joel B. Zayre. He was pronounced dead on arrival at the hospital.

I was treated for a flesh wound and for a broken collarbone and released. I remained at the hospital, however, to be with Steve. He'd been shot through the lung, and for the first forty-eight hours the doctors could offer little hope. Then he began to rally.

His mother and Livingston flew back to Chicago. They stayed until Steve was off the critical list. Then they returned to California.

For the past three weeks Steve has been at my apartment. He's recovered to the point where today I felt I could tell him what Rita has known for a month: that I have a very short time left in which to live.

He didn't take it very well at first. He was broken up and he was angry. It wasn't fair, he said. I told him that I'd thought the same thing at first—that I was being short-changed—but that I no longer did.

"But we've hardly got acquainted," he said.

"We've got acquainted pretty well, it seems to me," I replied.

He sighed unevenly.

"Actually," I went on, "it's your pulling through that's made the difference. If you hadn't, I probably would have continued to feel that I wasn't getting all I'm entitled to. Not only that, but I would have felt responsible for your death. In the hours while you were unconscious I kept bawling myself out for not having had sense enough to know that even if Pepper had been caught that night he wouldn't have been hauled right into a police lineup and that both of us wouldn't have had to rush down immediately to the station to identify him, or for not at least having checked first with the FBI. But that's water over the dam. You did pull through, and between us maybe we did something useful. Which is what it all boils down to in the end: doing something useful."

"But Pepper's pleaded not guilty."

"Don't let that worry you. He'll be convicted."

Steve looked skeptical, but I was positive that I was right. Burr had been over to see me several times, and Rita and I had been out to dinner at his house. He'd kept me posted, informally. The evidence against Pepper in Georgette's murder consisted of the bullets that had been found in the motel room. It was established that they came from the gun that had been recovered from the driveway beside the building I live in. The fingerprints on the gun matched the ones of Pepper which the FBI had in Washington and the ones which were taken when he was booked. In addition to that, there was Steve's testimony on Pepper's attempt to murder Georgette in California.

"He has a good lawyer," Steve pointed out.

I smiled. "Not as good as he might have had." According to Burr, Pepper had tried to hire Oscar Owen Nelson to defend him but Nelson had refused to take the case. Burr didn't know exactly why Nelson had refused but he was inclined to believe that Livingston had something to do with it, and I suspected that Burr was right. "Anyway, even if by some miracle Pepper should get acquitted of Georgette's murder, he'd still be nailed for twice trying to kill me." On those charges, the prosecution would have my deposition, for whatever it would be worth at the time, as well as eyewitness testimony from Mrs. Finnegan, Steve and the neighbors who'd watched from the building and from the street.

"Kohler hasn't talked yet, though."

"The police aren't through with him. Neither is his own lawyer. He's in so much trouble, what with murdering Zayre and taking a shot at the policeman who arrested him, that he'll eventually spill everything in order to get a lighter sentence. So will Sally Wayne. After all, she's charged with being an accessory."

"She didn't want to be, though. She was scared into it."

"So she claims. I don't think we'll ever know what her motives really were."

Steve turned away. "But you," he said unsteadily,"—you won't even be at the trial."

"Probably not." I put my arm on his shoulder. "I'll be spared that, for which I'm rather grateful."

He swallowed.

"There's a good and a bad side to everything," I added.

He shook his head.

"Yes, there is," I insisted. And I meant it. "I'm very satisfied at the moment." I meant that too.

He turned back to me. "But there's so much that's unfinished, Dad."

I looked at him. Although he still seemed young and vulnerable, he was much less so, I perceived, than he'd been two months before, and I was pleased by the change. "True," I said with a smile, "but if I lived to be a hundred there'd still be a lot unfinished." And maybe some of the things that I didn't finish, I amended silently, you will.

He tried to return my smile. He didn't quite succeed, but his expression did brighten. "Do you think they'll ever catch all the members of the gang?"

"Who knows? They've already caught some of them, Burr says, through the information they've got from Danner. And when Kohler talks, they may catch more. But all of them—perhaps not."

He nodded thoughtfully. "Is Mr. Burr going to be there tonight?"

"Yes. With his wife. And so are Ben Small and his wife. And so is Julie."

"Julie?"

"She's coming into town for the occasion." She'd visited Steve in the hospital, and according to Rita things were cooling off between Julie and Terry.

"That's great," Steve said.

It surely is, I thought. But I didn't say so. Rita and I had agreed that where Julie and Steve were concerned we'd let nature take its course. Besides, there wasn't time just then. I'd promised Rita that I'd drive her to the bakery to pick up the cake. She's giving a party tonight. It's my forty-third birthday.